The Blind Date Diaries

Dating? Lower than a bikini wax on my list of priorities.

Blind dating? Let's just say I'd rather have a Brazilian - and **not** the hot soccer player variety.

So the fact I've agreed to do a blind-date feature for *Pink*, the magazine I work for, and write it all up Bridget Jones style means one thing - *Pink* is in dire straits and this is my best shot at saving my job.

Make that my **only** shot because date number one is with Jack Reese – the son of the publisher of *Pink* – and he dislikes me as much as I dislike him.

Or at least I thought he did.

The Blind Date Diaries is a standalone enemies-to-lovers romantic comedy featuring a curvy heroine, a cocky carpenter with a crush and some genuinely cringe-worthy blind dates.

Keep in touch with Brenda St John Brown

Join Brenda's Book Babes
Get Brenda's Newsletter
Like Brenda
Follow Brenda on Bookbub
See what Brenda's reading on Goodreads
Follow Brenda on Amazon
Follow Brenda on Instagram

Also by Brenda St John Brown

A Brit on the Side
A Brit Unexpected
A Brit Complicated
Maid in England
Happy New You

Chapter One

ANGELINE

*I*t's been eight months and two days since I've had sex. Not that I'm counting, but if you give me a minute I could probably narrow it down to the hour. It's been *that* kind of dry spell.

And sure, for about seven months and six days I didn't mind. I didn't even really notice because I was nursing a broken heart/wounded ego. That will happen when you find sexts on your fiancé's phone to someone named Rachel. Problematic because my name is Angeline and *we were fucking engaged*. No, I wasn't snooping. Eli asked me to grab his phone from the coffee table where he left it and there they were on the screen. I'll spare you the gory details. Let's just say, a shit show ensued, ending with me leaving Manhattan and moving back "home" to upstate New York with my father so I could pay off my debt. Yes, rent-free living is A-MAZING. But honestly, what self-respecting thirty-two-year-old woman moves back in with her father without taking a serious blow to her pride? Not this one.

So the fact that my sex drive had all but parked? Not exactly a shocker. But sometime in the past few weeks, my libido has woken up again and I've been climbing out of my skin with need, want, lust – whatever you call it when you're horny as hell and don't even have a booty call in your contact list.

Which is still a pretty poor excuse for the fact that I'm teetering on the edge of hooking up with Jack Reese tonight. Because not only is he flirting hard, he is damn hot. And yes, that is the vodka talking because no way in hell would I admit it otherwise. If this place had a decent wine selection, I wouldn't be admitting it either. I can hold my Shiraz with the best of them. Vodka, not so much.

"Are you sure you want to encourage him?" My best friend and self-professed work wife, Melissa, tugs on the hem of my tank top as Jack goes to the bar to get me another drink. "I didn't even think you liked him very much."

"I don't have to like him to want him." In fact, it's easier that way. I tip the last of my vodka tonic into my mouth.

"You know, lots of people have a vibrator for this kind of thing." Melissa's mouth twists in a half-smile. "If you're too embarrassed to buy one yourself, I can get you one because that's the kind of friend I am."

I roll my eyes. "I've been wearing out my damn vibrator the past few weeks. I just need the real deal once and I'm sure I'll be fine."

"I don't know. What if you have Jack and you can never go back?" Melissa barks out a laugh. "It's possible, you know."

"I seriously doubt that."

Although an hour later when Jack's tongue is scraping along my collarbone, well... my vibrator doesn't do that, that's for sure. I'm pressed up against the counter in his kitchen and already writhing, my hands fisting his T-shirt. There's no AC in here and his skin is hot through the thin cotton, but when I try to lift it, he grabs my wrist.

"Patience, sweetheart." He sucks gently at the skin behind my ear, making me gasp.

"I don't want to be patient." I wrench my hand free. "Patience is for round two."

Jack's chuckle rumbles through his chest. "Is that so?"

"Unless you're a one and done type of guy?" I raise my eyebrows. "But I would have thought you're better than that."

"You would have thought right." Jack spins me around so my ass is pressed against him. He hikes my skirt up in one smooth motion and slips a finger inside my panties, letting it slide along my slick center. It's all I can do not to come on the spot.

"It's been a long time. I'm not sure you want to do too much of that." My words come out breathless and I moan as Jack slips one finger inside, then two. Holy. Shit. I grip the counter like it's a lifeboat and I'm about to drown.

"Are you wet because you want me or because it's been a long time?" Jack's voice is a low growl in my ear.

"Does it matter?"

Jack doesn't answer, just thrusts his fingers into me again, while circling my clit with his thumb. I gasp and he increases the pressure of his thumb. Part of me doesn't want to come this way – I came here for sex, dammit – but the other part of me is so eager, so ready, that if he doesn't stop in the next ten seconds, I'm going to...

"Christ, Jack. I told you I can't hold on." I squeeze my eyes shut as I ride the beginning of the wave.

"No one's asking you to, sweetheart." Jack's other hand moves up to my breast and pinches my nipple. And I come against his hand so hard it's a wonder I don't black out. As it is, I'm grateful his arm is still wrapped around me because even my arms are shaky gripping the countertop.

It's three deep breaths before I extricate myself from Jack's grasp and turn to face him. "Wow, that was um...wow."

"You didn't answer my question." One corner of Jack's mouth is turned up, but he doesn't look amused. Everyone says he looks like Henry Cavill, and I admit, I see it. But I see it a lot more when he keeps his mouth shut. Because when he speaks, he's pure Jack. Case in point? "Was it me you wanted, sweetheart? Or was I the most viable option?"

"You say that like we're finished." I raise my eyebrows.

"We might be." Jack's eyes narrow. Not a lot, but enough so I notice.

"Leaving yourself high and dry?" I glance down at the obvious tent in his shorts. "I didn't think that was your style."

"I don't usually fuck where I eat." Jack pauses, but not long enough for me to say anything. "But you seemed desperate."

"Asshole." Heat rises in my face, a mixture of anger and embarrassment.

"Hey, no judgment." Jack takes a step back and shoves his hands in his pockets. "I mean, we all have needs, right?"

"My God..." I stop because I don't even know how to finish that sentence. My God, I can't believe I just let you finger fuck me? My God, I can't believe I forgot who you actually are? And I let you finger fuck me? My God, I have to see you tomorrow— and every day for at least the next couple of weeks – and I let you finger fuck me?

I don't think I've said any of those things out loud, but I can't be sure because the next words out of Jack's mouth are, "Don't worry, sweetheart. This can be our little secret."

"You know what? I have to go." I reach for my bag on the counter and dig for my phone. "Let me call an Uber and I'll be out of here."

"I can take you home, Angeline." Jack's tone softens.

"No. You can't." I don't even remind Jack that we took an Uber here because we'd both been drinking. The truth is, he didn't have more than one – maybe two max – and for all I know his car is right outside and he's perfectly capable of driving it. I just grab my phone and open the app, keeping my eyes on the screen. It takes almost a minute for me to get a car because I fumble on the screen, but finally I book a driver – six minutes away – and look up at Jack's shoulder. "Done. I'll wait outside."

"Ang--" Jack starts then stops just as quickly. "You know what? If that's what you want, fine."

"I'll see myself out." I pull my bag onto my shoulder and make myself meet his eyes. "I'm not embarrassed about this, Jack. That said, I would appreciate keeping this just between us."

And Melissa because she knows I left the bar with Jack, but we live by the Girl Code.

"Who do you think I'm going to tell, sweetheart?" Jack raises an eyebrow at me.

"Guys at the office?" I swallow hard because I have to make myself say it so it's out there. On the record. "My boss?"

"Do you really think I'm going to tell my mother I finger banged you in my kitchen tonight?" Jack doesn't roll his eyes, but it's implied. "If I didn't tell her about Karen Kline putting her hands down my pants in the back of the bus in seventh grade, I'm sure as hell not going to tell her about this."

"I know. I just..." I stutter because I can't help it. I need my job as managing editor of *Pink* magazine and I need Victoria Buchanan (formerly Reese) to believe I'm cool and competent and in control. Pretty much exactly the opposite of how I've acted tonight. "This was a mistake and I don't want it to hurt me professionally."

"Like I said, it can be our little secret."

"Thank you. I appreciate that." I let out a long breath because judging by the look on Jack's face he means it.

"Always glad to be of service." Jack pauses. "Sweetheart."

God, I hate that tone. Ass hat.

I cross the kitchen and yank open the door leading to the stairs, letting my heels pound on the wooden steps as I clunk down them. Every step reverberates in my head and by the time I've reached the sidewalk in front of Jack's house, all the endorphins from my earlier orgasm have vanished.

It wasn't worth it. I let my body overrule my head and made the worst possible choice. The only worse one would be if I'd propositioned Victoria herself. Instead I picked her son – and now I'm going to have to trust that he's not going to make me look like a fool at the office. The sole saving grace is that we don't actually work together. He's a carpenter and is building display cases for the lobby area. It's not even like we need to speak to each other.

Yet, as I step into my Uber when it arrives, I glance up at the window and see Jack standing there. Watching me get in the car. And even though I think he's doing it to make sure I don't get mugged standing outside alone – fat chance because East Rochester is not a hotbed of criminal activity – my heart sinks. The reality is, I'm going to see him. Even if he wasn't doing a project at *Pink,* he's my boss's only son. He's generally around.

And my body, traitor that it is, will remember what happened tonight – and what didn't. It's going to wonder what it would have been like if that hard cock I felt pressed up against me ended up inside of me. No matter how much my head tells me I need to forget.

Chapter Two

ANGELINE

As far as I know, Jack has stayed true to his word. He's also stayed out of sight, although, unfortunately, not out of mind. Our little tryst sneaks into my head at odd moments – when I'm ordering lunch from the bagel place across the street, driving home from work, and yes, when I'm in bed. Alone. My vibrator stays locked in its drawer, not because I don't want the release it will bring, but because I don't want to have Jack in my head when I get it.

The only time I don't think of him is in the office. Ironic, I know, but for the first time since I've started working at *Pink*, I'm glad we're understaffed because I'm totally snowed under. Putting out a weekly magazine is no joke, even in a market like Rochester, New York. When Victoria swoops into my office and says we have a lunch meeting to talk about a new feature, I'm so frazzled I don't question it. Or check with Melissa to see if there's an agenda for the meeting in my calendar.

Rookie. Mistake.

Going to lunch with Victoria without an agreed-upon agenda almost always means she has an idea for a new feature that's bat-shit crazy enough for her not to want to bring it to a general staff meeting. The last time this happened I ended up doing a feature on Teacup Chihuahuas. Did you know that some breeders charge up to $11,000 for those dogs? Crazy, right? But not as crazy as Victoria's latest idea, which makes Teacup Chihuahuas look Pulitzer-worthy.

That *Pink* is in dire straits? I get it. As the managing editor, I see the revenue reports and can't help noticing their recent decline. That a blind dating feature could help bring in untapped advertising dollars? It's unconventional enough for *Pink* that it could be great. But that I'm the right person to do said dating feature? I'm not on board at all. Despite the certainty on my boss's face.

"You'll be perfect. People like you," says Victoria, flicking her fork over her plate. I haven't seen her eat anything, but that's pretty par for the course. I think her superpower is surviving on air. "Look how many letters we got after you went to that Rochester Women in Business gala on my behalf."

The letters we got were because *Pink* was there at all, and they were all along the lines of *Finally! The only women's magazine in upstate New York is actually attending an event honoring women*. It felt like a no-brainer to me, but to Victoria, it was a new and exciting opportunity. Well, no. Not so new or even very exciting, just an invitation Cath, the former managing editor of *Pink*, didn't find interesting enough to accept.

One of the many reasons she's the former managing editor, but I can't help thinking Victoria wouldn't dare ask Cath to do a blind dating feature. Cath was tall, glamorous, and imposing, much like Victoria herself, who, even in her late fifties, is more Anna Wintour than I'll ever be. I'm more like Anne Hathaway in *The Devil Wears Prada*. Pre-makeover. Although if I could afford a makeover, you bet your Chanel suit I'd do it.

I sigh and stab at my chicken, pausing before I take a bite to say, "How would it work?"

Victoria widens her bright green eyes and her eyebrows

disappear under heavy auburn bangs. Just when I think she's made of pure Botox, her face does something crazy and moves like it's supposed to. "We can work out the specifics, but I'm thinking something simple - readers nominate your date, you go on said date, and write about it. All those dating apps are so impersonal. Swipe right. Swipe left. This is almost retro, yes?"

Retro isn't the word I would choose, but I take that bite of chicken to buy myself time to think. Victoria has a lot of money, which is why she's the publisher of *Pink* in the first place, but her attention to detail leaves more than a little to be desired. Which is where the rest of the worker bees and I come in. Not that I mind – she hired me on the spot eight months ago when I was so desperate for a job I was seriously considering asking my brother, Theo, if he had any openings in his dental practice. I had even – shudder – started investigating qualifications to become a dental hygienist.

The thought sobers me. Spit, blood, and teeth with a side of halitosis or writing a blind dating feature? The choice is clear.

I nod at Victoria. "We need to capitalize on this by doing both online and print. Maybe have the nominations come in online and make the write-up exclusive to the print edition to encourage people to buy print?"

"I like that idea." Victoria nods and scrapes her fork along the rim of her plate. "And maybe we'll get some men interested, too, as they scope out their competition."

"We need to stick to our target demographic, which is women age twenty-five to fifty-four, or we'll lose focus." My tone is firm when I say this. *Pink* is struggling and trying to be all things to all people isn't the way to remedy that. We're a women's magazine selling the notion that maybe women really can have it all. And who knows? Maybe they can. I've seen no evidence, but that doesn't mean it's not possible, right?

"I'm not proposing we lose focus, Angeline. I'm proposing we use this feature and pull out all the stops because if we don't see a dramatic improvement, I'm going to be forced to take *Pink* down the online 'zine route." Victoria leans forward, pointing her fork at me to emphasize her words. "I don't want that, and I know you don't either, but what choice will I have?"

Victoria isn't one to make threats, so the fact that she's mentioning the online-only zine at all means she's thinking about doing exactly that. No more *Pink* in print, no more shiny pages, and most likely, no more need for a managing editor.

She could cut costs by using freelancers and a few good web developers. And I'd be in the same spot I was eight months ago when I moved back here – jobless, sans prospects, and panicked. The panic would be different now, but it's not like Rochester, New York is a hotbed of journalism jobs. I'd be begging Theo for a job faster than you could say Novocaine.

Or moving. Again. And while I have a vague plan to go back to New York eventually, I want it to be when I can use my managing editor title at *Pink* to land a decent job. That won't happen with less than a year of experience. Hell, moving back to New York without at least two years as managing editor means I'd be right back where I was when I left – making a barely livable wage as an associate editor at a big consumer magazine. Glamorous in theory, but in practice? Let's just say I had a favorite brand of instant ramen and my daily coffee was compliments of my corner bodega, not Starbucks. Eli, with his hedge fund manager's salary, was a Godsend. Until he wasn't. Obviously.

"So when do you want to start this?" I ask. "We need a snappy name and some great graphics first, and I'm sure Patrick will need some lead time."

"I'd like to start the feature next week, so a staff meeting as soon as possible wouldn't be out of order." Victoria stabs a piece of lettuce in her Caesar salad, but doesn't put it in her mouth. Instead she frowns – there go those eyebrows moving again – before glancing back up at me. "I know this feels like it's coming out of left field, but I've been getting a lot of pressure from Phil to retire so we can travel, and his case becomes much more compelling if the magazine is dying a painful death."

Phil is Victoria's...something. Partner? Boyfriend? Companion? She's been married a few times and says she'll never have another wedding, so I'm not sure of his label, but he's one of those distinguished older guys who has a tan year-round and wears boat shoes a lot. Melissa says he used to own a transportation company and is rich enough to buy half of Rochester. If he was the publisher of *Pink*, we'd have folded by now, but Victoria's adamant about keeping her work and love life separate. Which also means she's not going to get a last-minute save from Phil if *Pink's* downward spiral continues.

I muster up a wide smile. "Well, we'll just have to make sure the magazine lives another day."

Victoria smiles, too, although hers isn't as wide. "From your lips to God's ear."

The thing is, I don't think Victoria wants *Pink* to fold any more than I do. Travel with Phil would be amazing, but if she wanted to do it, she would have pulled the plug already. "So we need a name. What do you want to call this thing?" I ask.

"Something cute but not saccharine. It needs to have broad appeal. We want our twenty-somethings to be as eager to read about your dates as our bored housewives." Victoria pops the piece of lettuce into her mouth and chews for three seconds before saying, "Too bad *The Bachelorette* is trademarked."

"I'm going on a few blind dates, not looking for a husband." To be fair, I was never looking for a husband, even when Eli came along. But post-Eli, men are lower than a bikini wax on my list of priorities. "How about something like "Blind Dating for the Modern Woman"?"

"That sounds like something your grandmother would have read sixty years ago in *Good Housekeeping*. Right beside a feature about creative leftovers." Victoria gives me a steady stare that's way more effective in communicating her disdain for my idea than anything she could say.

"Okay, how about the "'Blind Date Diaries'"? Kind of like *Bridget Jones's Diary*, but I refuse to record my weight." I take another bite of chicken to emphasize the point. I like food and the one time I thought I wanted to be a size six, I realized pretty quickly food wasn't going to be part of that equation so there went that idea.

"The 'Blind Date Diaries'?" Victoria nods. "I like it. We can make the layout really pink and ask Patrick to throw some clip art hearts on the page?"

That sounds awful, but I nod. Patrick, the head of graphics, has a way of taking a vision and making it better than you thought it could be. "Sure. We'll see what he comes up with. Now all I have to do is find a date for diary entry number one." For next week. I could always ask my elderly widowed neighbor, Mr. Webster. He's cute in that way shuffling eighty-eight-year-old men are cute, and he likes me. Says I remind him of his granddaughter. I bet I could bribe him with cake and a promise to walk his dog?

"Well, I have a thought about that." Victoria's eyes drop and she takes another stab at her salad, which makes my palms go a little clammy. Victoria taking two bites of actual food in the course of a meal can only be bad news for me.

"Oookaay?"

"We need to front load this feature with a sure thing, so what do you think about Jack?" Victoria puts the lettuce in her mouth and chews, her lips pursing as she does it.

"Jack, as in your son, Jack?" As in the Jack who had me bent over his kitchen counter two nights ago? I'm amazed I'm not choking right now, that's what I think. I also think of his hand on my bare skin, which I'm sure isn't what Victoria was angling for when she asked the question.

"I know, readers might find that suspect, but we have

different last names, and I can't imagine anyone bothering to dig that deep." Victoria pauses, and her tone is careful as she continues, "I also know he can be a bit, well, rough around the edges, but he's polite and educated, and he'll be a good date."

Polite? Not the word I would use. Sexy, arrogant, and frustrating, on the other hand, are on the money. I see Jack's face turned up in a smirk as he calls me 'sweetheart' and I can't imagine going out on a date him. Even before the other night. So for us to go out on a date on which my job depends has disaster written all over it. But saying that to Victoria, who not-so-secretly thinks the moon rises and sets on her only son? Bigger disaster.

I take a deep breath. Then another because I can't get the words out. But when I do, they're strong and sound so genuine I almost believe them myself. "If he's game, I'll do it. I mean, why not, right?"

Besides the obvious reason, well... There's no reason not to. No reason at all.

Chapter Three

JACK

*A*voiding Angeline Sinclair doesn't mean she's not starring in my shower fantasies. Pathetic, I know, but I was too caught up in being a self-righteous prick the other night to finish what I started when the woman herself was ready, willing, and bent over my kitchen counter. I'm not even sure Angeline picked up on the self-righteous part, but she didn't miss my dick behavior. I made sure of that.

Which proves again that I should've given her what she came for because at least I wouldn't have left myself with a raging case of blue balls. And maybe I would've gotten her out of my system once and for all.

Because, yeah, I'm that guy. The guy who has a thing for the woman who hates him. It feels dumb to call it a crush. I'm thirty years old and "crush" is all teenage angst and shit. I didn't have much angst about it before Monday night, her dislike for me aside. Now...maybe it's a crush after all.

"Who the hell hooks up on a Monday night?" I ask my friend Chris, sitting across the table from me as I take a bite of my sesame bagel with melted Swiss. His bagel/sandwich place, Oh My Bagel, is across the street from *Pink* and I'm sitting here to delay going there. A tactic he's made clear he thinks is asinine.

"Hey, there are worse days. Like Wednesday. Brings new meaning to the idea of hump day, though." Chris grins. "You know you're going to have to pull up your socks and go over there, right?"

"Who says shit like that? Pull up my socks? Really?" I roll my eyes.

"Show her your sensitive side." Chris says. "From what you've said, she doesn't even know you have one."

That's because my first impression on Angeline was awful and, apparently, she's not one for second chances. My mother was having a ladies' luncheon at her Pittsford McMansion and I waltzed in – unshowered, unshaven, and dressed in dirty clothes after the power had been off at my place for three days. I'm not that much of an asshole. If I knew she was having a party, I wouldn't have gone. But my mother doesn't clear her social calendar with me, it was January, and I was sick of freezing to death in my apartment.

Mom was fine with me barging in – or at least as fine as she is when her plans are disrupted – but I was embarrassed as fuck. So I did what I do best and overcompensated. I sat down at the table next to Angeline, reached across her for a roll, and made a sarcastic comment when she recoiled.

Stellar start, right?

The thing is, the more I saw her around, the more I noticed her. The way her lips puckered a little when she was trying not to laugh. The curve of her shoulder. And yes, her ass. I'm an ass man. Sue me. I even had grand thoughts of asking her out properly. But she wrote me off as a jerk based on our initial meeting and I've played the part perfectly.

"Maybe I should –" I start.

"Darling. There you are. I was on my way up to see you." My mother pulls out the chair next to Chris and gives him a close-mouthed smile. "Christopher. It's always a pleasure. May I please have a black coffee? And what are your specials today?"

"For the vegetarians I have an It's All Greek To Me – feta, cucumber, tomatoes, black olives, and schmear of black olive cream cheese on a spinach bagel. But I see you going for That's Some Spring Chicken, which is grilled chicken, spring onions, ranch dressing, and arugula on a cheese bagel." Chris rises from his chair. "Can I get you one on the house?"

"No thank you. I have a lunch meeting, but Phil was asking." Mom gives a vague wave of her hand. "I'll text him and let him know."

She makes no move toward her phone, which means Chris and his specials will be out of mom's head before she walks out the door. On the one hand, she's got a great head for business. *Pink* was her baby and she's built it up from nothing. On the other, she loses her reading glasses almost every other day. Mostly when they're propped on top of her head.

"Speaking of lunch, my break is almost over." I point to my empty coffee cup. "Did you need something or were you coming by *Pink* to check on my progress?"

"I was actually coming by *Pink* because I have a proposition for you." Mom eyes me like she's looking over her reading glasses, even though she doesn't have them on.

"A proposition." I raise my eyebrows in a silent question. I know better than to even say okay when she looks at me like that, in case she takes it as assent.

"We're trying a new feature for the magazine called the "Blind Date Diaries". Sort of a *Bachelorette*-Lite, with Angeline as the bachelorette." Mom pauses and I still don't say anything, but the minute she says the A-word, you bet my attention is riveted. "We want the series to kick off quickly, which means fudging the first date a bit. That's where you come in."

"Me?" I'm not stupid. I know where my mother is going with this. But I'm going to need her to spell it out.

"As Angeline's first date." Mom sits back in her chair and clasps her hands together. I'd bet a custom dining room set she has no clue about my feelings for Angeline, but you wouldn't know it by the Cheshire cat expression on her face.

"Does she know about this?" I can't imagine her reaction, but something along the lines of 'when hell freezes over' comes to mind.

"We had lunch yesterday." Mom nods. "She's on board."

Okay, that's a surprise. Next question. "Why me?"

"Why not you?" Mom smiles. "You're fabulous and I think you'd be a good match."

She doesn't mean it *that* way. But I can't help but say, "I think you might be the only one who thinks so."

"Angeline had no objection." Mom's eyebrows go up, even though she didn't phrase it as a question.

"None?" I lean forward in my chair. I might look overeager, but this is important.

"I mean, she didn't want to record her weight, but that wasn't on the table, was it?" Mom scoffs.

"I don't even know what that means." I hold up my hand as she opens her mouth to explain. "But whatever. The "Blind Date Diaries"? What do I have to do, exactly?"

"Take her on a date. The bulk of the work lies with her."

"Okay." That's not how dating works in my experience, but a thought occurs to me that's suddenly more pressing. "If I do this, though, we're even."

"Even?" My mother says the word like she's not sure what it means.

"I'm paid in full." I make myself hold my mother's gaze, which is harder than normal. "No more holding the business loan you gave me over my head. Either this makes us even or you let me pay you back in cash."

"Don't be ridiculous, Jack. That was a gift." My mom waves her hand like the topic is finished.

But not with me, it's not. "It was a gift with strings attached. While I'm grateful you helped me get my design business off the ground, I need to run it my way."

Which means no more random redesign of my business cards, for starters. I like a script font as much as the next guy – so basically not at all – yet that was my mom's recent contribution to Jack Reese Designs. To the tune of a thousand printed cards charged to my damn account that are only going to be used for a bonfire one of these days.

"I'm just trying to help. You may or may not have noticed, I've run a successful business of my own for quite some time." Mom's tone hardens.

"I know, and I appreciate all you've done for me." I dig my knuckle into my thigh so my voice stays even. "But I've been doing this for six years now, and I need Jack Reese Designs to reflect Jack Reese, not Victoria Buchanan."

I also should have had this conversation with my mother a while ago, but the ten thousand dollars she lent me back in the day is a persuasive argument for letting her have her say. Sure, I've made her a bunch of custom pieces and probably paid her back and then some, but the truth is, it's always felt like the scales tipped in her favor.

"So you're proposing that you go out with Angeline in exchange for me staying out of your business?" Mom rolls her eyes a little. "Both literally and figuratively?"

I know she's giving me a chance to back out, but I can't. I won't. "Yep, pretty much."

My mother spends a solid minute studying me. It's an old trick of hers that worked when I was a teenager. Now? Not so much. I stay so still I could be mistaken for the chair I'm sitting in.

"Fine." Mom nods once. "The date will be Friday. Afterwards, Angeline will write it up as a diary entry for *Pink*. Since we're using this to boost revenue, she'll sell the date, the place, and the series in her write-up without making it read like she's selling it at all."

"Friday?" My eyebrows go up. I'll think more about Mom's agreement later. "As in three days from now? Is there a date already arranged then?"

"Well, no. Of course not." Mom's brow furrows. "That's your job."

My mind races. "Where am I supposed to take her?"

"That's up to you, Jack." The furrow in Mom's brow deepens. "I'm sure you'll think of something."

I will. I mean, obviously I will. If I'm really doing this. Am I really doing this? I want to be free and clear of my so-called debt, but damn if I'm not second-guessing it. "Are you sure I'm the right choice to do this for *Pink*?"

"Well, I think so." She pauses. "Is there a reason you don't?"

Besides the fact that Angeline thinks I'm an asshole and I've blown every opportunity I've ever had with her?

Aloud I say, "Nope. I'm sure it will be great."

"I am, too. Just ask her what she likes," Mom says, picking up her coffee. "It's not like it's a true blind date. She knows you."

That's the thing. She doesn't. But she thinks she does. And this might just be my opportunity to prove her wrong.

Chapter Four

ANGELINE

he idea of going on a date with Jack Reese has been making my stomach clench, but not nearly as much as this staff meeting to introduce the "Blind Date Diaries", with everyone around the table talking at once. Victoria was supposed to be here, but "something came up" so I'm flying solo and floundering. So far, it's going as badly as I imagined it would. The only people who are sitting back quietly are Patrick, the graphics guy, and Melissa. Although their expressions speak volumes and I'm pretty sure they're both saying, *Better you than me.*

"You're going on blind dates our readers pick for you?" Beth, the staff writer, looks down at the page in her hand and back up at me. "Why?"

"Advertising-wise, this is a month-long segment, is that right?" asks Mike, one of the two advertising sales guys.

"And Patrick's on point for the graphics?" asks Erin, the head of marketing. "I mean, that's fine, but I've got some other stuff in the queue for him and I really wish you'd have spoken to me first.

"What kind of support are you looking for from an IT

perspective?" asks Ravi, the computer tech. "Because we need to make sure the website can handle more traffic."

The voices swirl around the conference room and I feel the pressure build in my chest. When I agreed to launch the segment this week, I ran with it, mocking up a sample with Patrick's help on the graphics. I didn't think about all the moving parts required to bring a new feature to life. *Because I've never been in charge of a big feature.* When I was an editorial assistant at *Lush*, I thrived on bringing new ideas to the table but was never senior enough to execute. Since I've been in charge at *Pink*, I've played it safe, keeping to the status quo.

And look where that's gotten us. Nowhere.

I look at the staff gathered around the table, gauging their eyes and the set of their jaws. I see uncertainty – Beth; some annoyance – Erin; and a little bit of panic – Ravi. What I don't see is excitement, which makes my heart sink. If I can't even get the staff excited about this, how are we going to sell it to *Pink's* readers?

Before I can second-guess myself, I put my fingers in the corners of my mouth and whistle – one benefit of having a dad who's a former basketball coach and two older brothers. They made sure I knew how to damn well whistle. The chatter stops immediately, all eyes trained on me.

I clasp my hands together in front of my chest. "Everyone's got some great questions, and I'm going to address them all. I'll be meeting with each department individually today to talk about how we can support the new feature, but remember, it's only one feature. Yes, it's an important one because of the tie-in with the print edition, but it doesn't mean everything else takes a back seat either."

"I still don't understand why we're doing this," says Beth. "It's not on brand at all."

Beth's tone is defiant and a little bit whiny, and my instinct is to say something about how we're trying to expand and diversify. Basically a 'suck it up, buttercup', but nicer. But then I look at Ravi and Erin, and even though they didn't ask the question, they're interested as hell in the answer.

I take a deep breath and my voice is low when I speak. "We're doing this because if we don't − or if we don't do something equally drastic − we're going to lose the print edition and be relegated to the status of an online zine that can run almost solely on freelance contributions with a digital editor at the helm. Honestly, that digital editor won't be me. I daresay it won't be anyone in this room, and it might not be anyone in this city. Because it's digital and as long as the content is semi-relevant, all the editor has to do is compile. *Pink* as we know it will cease to exist and I, for one, want to do everything in my very limited power to make sure that doesn't happen."

Plus, dear God, I can't face working in a dentist's office.

"So you're saying we're in danger of losing print?" Mike straightens in his chair.

I make sure to meet his gaze. "Not necessarily, but we need to turn this around and Victoria feels time is of the essence."

The room goes so still I can hear Patrick breathing at the other end of the table when I finish. I didn't mean to say that. Not in such stark terms anyway. For a few seconds, I let the panic bubble in my chest. I'm supposed to be a leader. The surest way to make sure everyone's polishing up their resumes is to drop this type of bomb because I'm not the only person in this room who needs a job. We all do. Even if we save print, it won't do us any good if we don't have staff.

Then Melissa says, "Angeline is determined we're not going to let that happen. And I admit, I thought it was a whacky idea, but then I came across this." She holds up a copy of *The Ratings Guidebook*, a media bible of sorts that ranks television shows by popularity. "Guess what shows consistently rank in the top five? *The Bachelor* and *The Bachelorette*. People want this kind of entertainment. It lets them feel like they're peering in the window of a possible happily-ever-after. I mean, do you know how many people vote for who gets a rose in these shows? Millions."

"So Ang is going to be *Pink's* own *Bachelorette?*" Erin's tone is snarky, and I dig my fingernails into my palm to keep myself from snapping back at her. Just because I'm curvy doesn't mean I couldn't be a Bachelorette.

"Without the roses. Because that's dumb, man. I don't care what anyone says," says Patrick, with an exaggerated eye roll.

Everyone laughs and I shoot Patrick a grateful look. I owe him big time for jumping on board with this and keeping any doubts he's had to himself. "The introductory spread is going in the print edition, we've got banner ads for the website, and Patrick's also put together a set of social media banners. We'll need to really build buzz about this before we run the first blind date story next week."

"What if no one responds?" asks Mike. "You're relying on nominations, right? What if there aren't any?"

"Oh, come on. As if." Melissa side-eyes Mike and everyone laughs.

I laugh, too, but the truth is, Mike just hit on my biggest fear related to this whole thing. Not the dates themselves because if I can get through lunch with Victoria, I can get through a blind date. But what if no one wants to participate? What if no one wants to go out with me?

And I know it's not about *me* at all in the broad scheme of things. But in the details, it is. I'm the datee in this thing and I'm no Helen of Troy. I mean, I'm not ugly, just...average. Average height. Average looks. On the plus side, I have great cheekbones. On the minus side, I'm carrying at least twenty extra pounds because I don't exercise enough. My other older brother, Will, always says I have the body of a supermodel hidden in me somewhere, but Will's a personal trainer and he gets paid to say things like that.

Erin's voice snaps me out of my reverie. "We need a plant."

"A plant?" A shrub, maybe a rhododendron? "For what?"

"Not that kind. I mean a pre-determined winner for date one," says Erin. "So in case no one comes forward, we can fudge it and have someone to kick this off."

Before I can respond, a voice rings out from the back of the room and all heads turn towards Jack Reese, who's somehow slipped in the back when no one was watching. "I'll do it."

My heart leaps to my throat. Jack's gaze is cool and detached, although his eyes rake over me like he's picturing my gray skirt pushed up around my waist and now I can't help imagining that, too. I glance down at my fingers twisting the pen in my hand and when I glance back up at Jack, I see a trace of a smirk on his lips. Like he knows he's had an effect on me and he's ticking off some mental scorecard.

"Uh, yeah?" My words are no better than a stutter. "I mean, that could work, right?"

"Unless you have a better suggestion?" Erin's tone makes it clear what she thinks the likelihood of this is.

All eyes turn towards me. I could admit right now that the whole Jack thing has already been arranged, but it occurs to me that it probably looks better for Jack to offer, so I say, "Nope. Jack, that makes you bachelor number one. As long as you're up for it?"

"Oh, I'm up for it." Jack wriggles his eyebrows and Erin giggles.

I bite my lip, hoping it looks more like a smile than a grimace, as Patrick pushes his chair back and says, "If you sort that out, I'll put together a couple of layouts with the mock text, so we can see which one is more visually appealing. Once we have a template, the rest is easy, man."

Ravi nods and says something about traffic and the server, but I don't hear him because my attention is riveted on Jack, who's smiling at something Erin said. He looks the same –

faded T-shirt and shorts, brown hair slightly too long, curling at the ends. He looks the same as he did the last time I saw him, except for the way he's grinning at Erin. Like a puppy at a bone.

He laughs at something she says and it stabs me in the gut. I pick up my pile of folders and make a quick exit before I have to witness more of their flirting. And before I have to think about why it bothers me.

Chapter Five

ANGELINE

I t takes Jack ten minutes after the staff meeting ends to make his way to my office. I know because I'm alternating checking my watch with clenching my fists. Every time I hear Jack's laugh ring out across the office, I dig my fingernails into my palm a little more. It's a good thing he comes over when he does because I'm about two more of his loud guffaws away from drawing blood.

He leans against the doorframe, his voice low and rough like he spent last night and a good part of this morning smoking, drinking, and fucking – and not necessarily in that order. For all I know, he probably did. "Angeline. It is a pleasure to see you again."

"Come in and close the door." I pause for a breath. "Please."

Jack wriggles his eyebrows. "Well, darling, we might want to wait until after working hours. People talk, you know."

"Jack." My jaw tightens and I force a deep breath in through my nose. "Come in and close the damn door."

He laughs, but he does it, coming in and sprawling in one of the leather chairs in front of my desk. "What's got your panties in a twist today? You weren't this prickly the other night."

"What are you doing here?" I cross my arms over my chest.

"I heard you need a date. The print edition has one foot in the grave and I'm your white knight. Hell, I'm even willing to be photographed."

"How big of you." I shake my head. "But that still doesn't explain what you're doing in my office."

"I'm technically working for *Pink* right now. You remember I'm building some killer display cases in the lobby? I think you've walked by me a time or ten." Jack shakes his head, but his gaze sharpens as his eyes travel over my face. "You look stressed, Ang. Work getting you down? Or are you still sexually frustrated? We can talk about it if you'd like?"

"No." I cross my arms over my chest. Deliberately this time. "Did Victoria suggest you swoop in and figuratively pee on everything or do you need something?"

"I didn't realize you thought as little of my mother as you do of me." Jack shakes his head like I'm an errant school child. "Does she know?"

"Your mother is fine." She drives me crazy, but I'm not telling her son that. "It's you, and the fact that you're in my office without a valid reason or an appointment, that's the problem."

"I told you why I'm here." Jack leans back further in his chair. If he reclines any more, he's going to slide right off.

"To be my white knight?" My heart sinks because, dammit, that's exactly what he's going to be if he goes on this blind date.

The look on his face confirms it. "My mother said you need a sure thing to kick this off. So here I am."

"Yes, she mentioned you're going to be my sure thing." I scowl a little, but I don't care. "God help us both."

"Oh, come on. You're assuming I'm a terrible date, but I'm not as bad as you think." Jack rolls his eyes. "Not that you have anything to base your assumptions on."

"Gee, Mr. I-Don't-Fuck-Where-I-Eat, I can't imagine where

I got the idea you might be a less than perfect date." I dig my fingernails into my palm again and continue before Jack can respond. "I need this feature to be the biggest success *Pink* has ever had, and I'm not sure you and I are the right combination."

"Fine. No skin off my back either way." Jack shrugs. "Do you want to tell my mother you're having second thoughts or shall I?"

Shit. Telling Victoria that Jack is a no-go as my first date won't go over well. For whatever reason, she wants Jack to do this, and my protest – on the grounds I'd rather insert needles in my eye after all than go out with her son – is a giant check in the career-suicide column. But that doesn't mean I can't ask her why.

"I need to speak to her before this conversation goes any further." I flash a close-mouthed smile at Jack. "If you wait outside, I'll let you know when I've finished."

"You can go ahead and call in front of me. I promise to be on my best behavior."

A scream lodges itself in my throat. Jack's not stupid. He knows exactly what he's doing; if I insist on him leaving while I call Victoria, he has the opportunity to play victim. *Oh, Mom, I tried to convince her, but she's so unreasonable.* But if I call with him sitting in that chair with that expression on his face, I run the risk of letting Victoria know exactly how much her son can get under my skin.

It's a lose-lose, but I'd rather Jack be angry with me than Victoria because she's the one signing my paycheck. I point to the door. "Out. Please. Go flirt with Erin or something."

"Fine." Jack rises from the chair, pulling himself up to his full height, stretching like a peacock fanning its plume. He's tall and broad, his shoulders pulling against the seams of his T-shirt. He turns slowly – in case I want to ogle his backside? – and pulls the door open, leaving without a word. And, okay, I confess. I ogle a little, watching until he's halfway to the kitchen before picking up my phone.

Victoria answers on the second ring. "Angeline, has Jack been there yet?"

"He has, actually. That's why I'm calling." I take a deep breath to continue.

But Victoria beats me to it. "Terrific. I suggested he stop by to see you."

I'm dying to ask Victoria why she did that without warning me, but I bite my tongue, saying instead, "I've been thinking about how Jack's supposed to be my first date. I mean, the whole point is to get the readers involved in nominating potential dates, which is difficult to do if I already have one."

"Of course. Jack will be nominated like everyone else. The only difference is we already know he'll win. The timeframe is too tight to leave it to chance." Victoria's voice has a note of finality to it.

It's one I've learned to heed. But I can't resist asking, "Why does Jack want to do this? It doesn't really seem like his cup of tea."

"I think you'll have to ask Jack that yourself. But suffice it to say, he's committed to providing a story-worthy blind date."

My heart drops. "What does that mean?"

Victoria's laugh trills down the line. "I don't know, but I'm sure you're in good hands."

Famous last words. Of course Victoria would think that. She sounds so sure that anything I say now will only be perceived as nerves on my part or, worse, attraction. I say the only thing I can. "Yes, I'm sure I am, too."

We hang up and I stare at my desk phone for a solid minute until I hear a quick knock on my office door. I look up and Jack's standing there, one hand on the doorframe, the other on the handle. I nod and he pushes the door open but doesn't enter. He raises his eyebrows at me in a question, but before he can say anything that might force the scream lodged in my throat to escape, I say, "Our date is this Friday. Let me know where and when I'm supposed to meet you."

"No luck getting out of this with Mother Dearest then?" Jack asks.

"I didn't try. We both know this is the only way I'll ever go out on a real date with you, and if you're so desperate that you're willing to do this? Who am I to deny you the pleasure?" I sound more confident than I feel, which isn't a bad thing. I even manage a toothy fake smile at the end.

"Who, indeed?" Jack laughs before saying, "I'll text you, sunshine."

Sunshine? Really?

I smile in spite of myself as he walks away and cross the room to close the door behind him. I don't need Jack Reese to see my smile and take it as encouragement. That wouldn't be good for either one of us.

Chapter Six

JACK

The benefit of owning my own business – besides the nonexistent wardrobe requirements – is working my own hours. Not surprisingly, it's also the curse. Case in point: a couple of hours work at Oh My Bagel building an outdoor seating area has turned into an afternoon, bleeding into early evening. I quoted three hours, so now I'm eating the extra time, which sucks.

The only good thing is Chris has pitched in so we can finish the railing, and he's made a couple of monster bagel sandwiches that are the best thing I've had all week. I take a giant bite of my roast beef on a garlic bagel and mayo runs down my chin. Wiping it away, I say, "You need to put this on the menu. It's the best sandwich of my life, I shit you not."

Chris laughs. "Too bad your mix of pickles, onions, Thousand Island dressing, and mayo wouldn't work for most people. Although, we could call it Beef Around the Bush and add sprouts and lettuce so it lives up to the name. It would be a great rec for everyone avoiding their expense reports."

"I like the name." I take another bite, as if to prove it. "You should do it."

"Everyone wants standard turkey, lettuce, tomato, mayo. Trust me. I'm actually thinking about discontinuing the sandwich of the day because it's disheartening." Chris laughs again. "And when a sandwich becomes disheartening, it's a sign you're too invested and it's time to step away from the deli meat."

"I get that." I have to grin. Chris has an off-the-wall sense of humor, which is half the reason I do jobs for him despite the crap pay. The other half is that he's generous as hell and for every cent he doesn't pay me, he gives to charity – leftover food to the homeless shelter and at least one Habitat for Humanity project every summer. We met doing a Habitat house last summer when he was just getting Oh My Bagel off the ground. I worked for him for free then, and even though he pays me a little now – in both food and actual cash – his construction skills are still pretty awful.

I point to the piece of rail he's about to drive the last nail into. "You need a level. That's crooked as hell."

Chris backs up and looks at it, stepping into the road. "Why does my part look like it was done by my eight-year-old nephew? And why does Pittsford have such asshole regulations that outdoor dining needs to be enclosed anyway? Whatever happened to throwing a bunch of tables and chairs out onto the sidewalk?"

"It's not aesthetically pleasing." My mother's face comes into my head. She'd support a town ordinance requiring orderly table arrangements quicker than you could say HGTV.

"Do people care? Do you care when you come to have your bagel and coffee on a Saturday morning if it's aesthetically pleasing?" Chris shakes his head. "My customers care about caffeine first and food second. Aesthetics are so far down the list they're invisible."

"Well, maybe you'll expand your clientele." I hammer in another nail. The other restaurants have black metal foldable fencing, but Chris is doing it on the cheap, so we're making do with recycled timber from a job I did at the University of Rochester a few weeks ago. I was going to make a table out of it until I quoted Chris's job the other day, and it turned out he could either pay for materials or pay for labor. "There's lots of money in this corner of town. No reason you can't have a little more of it with your aesthetically pleasing outdoor dining area."

Chris throws his head back and laughs and I join in. It's not even that funny, but we're both laughing like idiots when the door to the office building across the street opens and out walk Angeline and Melissa. I haven't seen Angeline since I did that dick swinging through her office. Which, regardless of whether I was nervous or not, was a shit move. *Pink* is her house and I went in and pissed all over the floor like a drunken frat boy. With my usual dose of swagger to go along with it.

My laugh fades as Angeline and Melissa stop on the sidewalk. Angeline's wearing a black sleeveless sheath dress and stiletto sandals that make her legs look a mile long. She's not a tall woman, so that's probably the point. Add in her dark blonde hair swept up off her neck in one of those messy buns women seem born being able to do and she's hotter than hell. Melissa's smokin' and she knows it – today and every day. Her hair is shorter than mine and right now she's wearing a big flowy dress with some kind of African print and gigantic gold hoops. And totally pulling it off, judging by the way Chris's eyes are glued to her cleavage when I glance over at him.

I nudge his elbow just as Melissa notices us. She checks for cars and crosses the street, calling out, "Hey, are you going to have an outdoor patio now?"

Chris is still staring at Melissa's chest, so I answer. "It's an enclosure, according to town regulations."

Melissa turns to Angeline, who follows several steps behind. I think she might walk faster to her own execution. "Hey, Ang, lunch on the patio tomorrow?" To me she says, "Will it be done by then?"

I nod, keeping my eyes on Melissa as Angeline stops a couple steps behind. "It will be done in an hour, hopefully."

Especially considering it's nearing seven o'clock and will be dark in two.

"I like the wood you're using. It's different." Melissa grins. She has a great smile and the thought flits through my head that doing this blind date thing with her would be so much easier, and not only because she doesn't hate me. I can actually talk to Melissa like a normal human being, and it would still tick the paid-in-full box with my mom. I mean, that's why I'm doing this.

Partly. Sort of.

Okay, not really. But still.

Angeline nods and her gaze slides over me to land on Chris. "It looks really great. I'm sure it will be a big hit."

If I were a better man, I'd let Ang's comment go. I mean, Chris has a hammer in his hand like I do and it's his restaurant. There's no harm in anyone thinking this is mostly Chris's work and I'm just helping instead of the other way around. I'm obviously not the bigger man. Or even pretending to be. "I brought the timber over from a job I did at U of R and hinged it together so Chris can fold it up at the end of the day."

"Well, Pittsford takes its regulations pretty seriously," Angeline says as her eyes meet mine. Her eyes are gorgeous. The kind of green you'd find between Argyle and Lucky Green on the Sherwin Williams paint spectrum.

And yes, I've thought about it enough to settle on that description. Occupational hazard.

"They really do." I force my gaze down to the hammer in my hand and then over to Chris, who's still tongue-tied by Melissa's cleavage from the looks of things. "We should get back to work if your patio is going to be open tomorrow."

Chris gives a quick shake of his head. Finally. "It needs to be open tomorrow. You ladies should stop by for lunch. On the house, of course."

Angeline and Melissa both smile and Melissa says, "How about we stop by for lunch and pay so you can pay this guy?" Melissa tilts her head my way. "Word on the street is he's got a hot date tomorrow."

Truth: I haven't blushed since seventh grade and the whole Karen Kline in the back of the bus thing.

Also, truth: I'm blushing now and so is Angeline.

Chris's eyes dart between the two of us and he says, "So, you two..."

Angeline cuts him off. "It's not what you think." Her eyes meet mine again for a fraction of a second and then dart away as she says, "I got your text, by the way."

"Funny, I didn't get your reply." My tone has an edge to it, which I instantly regret. Damn, insecurity is a needy bitch. My smartass default needs a major makeover before tomorrow if I'm going to stand a chance with this woman.

Angeline's face hardens and this time she meets my gaze without blinking. "I've been in meetings all day. Working." She pauses and I half-expect her to ask if I know the definition of the word despite the tools in my hand. Instead she says, "I'll see you tomorrow at six. Consider this my reply."

She turns away and Melissa waits a few seconds before following, calling out a goodbye as she and Angeline cross back over the road and turn down the alleyway leading to the parking lot.

Chris waits until they're out of sight before asking, his voice low, "Really, man? I hope to God you know that's not the way to get the girl?"

"Yep." I pound my hammer into the top of the post, even though it's finished. I'm doing the same thing I always do when it comes to Angeline Sinclair. E.g. overcompensating for my feelings for her by pretending I have none.

I have twenty-four hours to figure out how to break the cycle.

Chapter Seven

ANGELINE

"*I* don't understand your animosity towards him. I mean, he's hot," says Melissa, taking another slice of pizza from the open box on my coffee table. Well, technically my father's coffee table, but who's quibbling over details?

"To start, he's arrogant and presumptuous. You heard him earlier." I lower my voice to imitate Jack. "'Funny, I didn't get your reply.' My God, if I want that level of BS, I'd call Eli."

"And hell would freeze over." Melissa laughs. "For what it's worth, I don't think he was trying to be a jerk."

"Really? So it just came naturally?" I let out a huff of frustration. "Every time I see him, I get a face full of Reeseitude."

Melissa giggles. "Have you ever thought that maybe he doesn't know how to act around you, so he reverts to what he knows?"

"No, because last I checked, we weren't twelve." I take a bite of my pizza so I won't resort to sixth-grade name calling. Not that Melissa would judge me for it, but she's way nicer than me, and I kind of want to rise to her level instead of convincing her to sink to mine.

"Except for the other night – which was clearly a break in

the space-time continuum – you and Jack have this conditioned response around each other that doesn't allow for any other kind of interaction."

"You mean, kind of like you and Chris? He ogles, you flirt, and never the two shall meet?" I raise my eyebrows and reach for the wine. I found a great Sicilian Nero d'Avola the other day, and even though it feels indulgent to have it with pizza, it's too good to pass up.

Melissa holds out her glass for a refill as she tries not to smile. "I'm on a dating sabbatical, remember?"

Melissa said back in February she's not dating for six months and it's June now. "So if he asks you out in August, you'll say yes?"

"I don't know. We'll see what happens in August." Melissa takes a sip of wine. "This is amazing, by the way. I can always count on you for the best wine."

"Don't thank me. Thank Eli." I roll my eyes and lower my voice. "'It's important to cultivate your palette, darling, and you're not going to do that with Two Buck Chuck.'"

Melissa covers her mouth to keep from spitting out her wine while she laughs, then says, "At least Jack seems like he'd go for Two Buck Chuck."

"I know. But, sadly, I wouldn't. Not anymore." I smack myself in the forehead. But lightly because it's just for effect. "Tell me again why I'm going out with Jack?"

"Well, you told me that Victoria –"

"Stop it. You know what I mean." I lean back against Dad's Pottery Barn couch cushion and close my eyes for one long minute. If someone had told me this time last year I'd be back in upstate New York, living with my father and planning a date with Jack Reese to try to save my job, I'd have laughed. And not a nice laugh either. I'd have laughed with a healthy side of haughtiness because New York City me thought things were pretty damn good and staying that way was a sure thing.

Further proof that New York City me was even more deluded than I'd realized. But at least I've been humbled, right? I open my eyes and ask Melissa, "What am I going to do?"

"Go out with Jack. Write a kickass piece about it to start off the series. Save the future of *Pink* as we know it." Melissa widens her eyes. "You're not the only one who needs this job, you know. Mike's got kids and Patrick needs to fund his weed habit."

"Patrick has a weed habit? Is it bad?" I straighten. I rely on Patrick a lot and if he has a problem...

"No. Maybe?" Melissa laughs. "I don't know if he even has a weed habit, but no one's that laid back in real life. My point is that you're not the only one with your job on the line. We all need this feature to succeed."

"I know. You're right." I squeeze my eyes shut for five seconds, then put my plate on the floor. "So first things first. Help me figure out what I'm going to wear."

"Let me see Jack's text again?" Melissa asks, holding her hand out for my phone. I dig it out from between the couch cushions and hand it over. She takes it and says, "You really should put a password on this. Okay, let's see. Texts. Jack Reese. *I'll pick you up tomorrow from the office at six. Dress casually.* You didn't ask him for any more details, did you?"

"No. I didn't want to encourage him, but now that means I have no idea what casual means."

"You could always text him back and ask, you know." Melissa suggests. "Casual can mean anything from shorts and a T-shirt to a skirt with flats instead of heels."

"I know, but..." I don't know how to articulate my hesitation. It's hard enough explaining it to myself, so my words sputter out. "We had that run-in earlier at Oh My Bagel, so now I can't text him without looking like a jerk. And double checking what to wear makes it look like I'm thinking about this as an actual date. He would love that, and I don't want to give him the satisfaction."

"So you don't want to give him the satisfaction of admitting you're thinking about this as a date, even though you're thinking about this as a date?"

"No. It's not a date. At least not a real one. And before you start psychoanalyzing, stop. There's nothing behind it, except that I don't want to go out with him. I'm doing it, but I'm not going to give him any more to gloat about than I already have." The other night in his kitchen gives him plenty.

"Fair enough." Melissa hands my phone back to me. "But you still want to look killer, obviously."

"Obviously." I put my phone face down on the couch and take a swallow of wine. "Does that make me shallow?"

"Are you kidding? It makes you human." Melissa laughs, then looks at the ceiling for a second. "So, if I were you, I'd wear your dark jeans with that yellow silk tank top you've got because the jeans look great on you and the yellow brings out your eyes. Then you can wear the sandals you wore to work today if you want to, or even those chunky brown ones if you think heels are too dressy. It's supposed to be in the eighties tomorrow, so jeans might be hot, but better safe than sorry in case you end up doing something weird."

"Oh my God. What do you mean by something weird?" What if Jack plans something off-the-wall just to goad me? "I should have asked to preapprove the date, shouldn't I?"

"No, you shouldn't have. I was joking." Melissa grins. "But in case you go off the beaten path, jeans are a safe bet."

"I can't even tell you how much I don't want to go off the beaten path with Jack Reese."

"It will be fine. Remember, Victoria is behind this and if he blows it, there goes his allowance," Melissa says.

"Do you think he really gets an allowance?" Judging by the

little of Jack's apartment I saw, construction either pays better than I think or Victoria's bankrolling him.

"I think you're losing focus. Jeans? Yellow tank top? Yes or no?"

I nod. "With my espadrille wedges. I like that idea, and I can wear those clothes to work since it's Friday."

"No." Melissa's lips form a perfect *O* as she shakes her head. "I know you don't want to put any effort into this, but at least wear a different blouse to work."

"Why?"

"Because the psychology of going out on a date includes getting ready for it. And if you're spending five minutes in the ladies' room fixing your makeup and heading back out the door, you're not in date mode, ready to have fun."

"But I have no intention of being in date mode." I furrow my brow. "This is work, and on top of that, I'm going out with Jack."

"Maybe, but your job for the duration of the "Blind Date Diaries" is to make it sound fun – or at least funny." Melissa winces a little as she continues, like she's bracing herself to walk across a floor covered in glass. "You need guys to go out with you and their sisters, best friends, or colleagues to nominate them. If you come across as a bitch at the beginning, no one's going to sign up for round two. The "Blind Date Diaries" will be dead in the water and drown *Pink* with it."

Ouch.

I bite my tongue so I don't say anything I might regret. Which is harder than it should be, because one of the reasons Melissa and I are such good friends is that she doesn't tell me what I want to hear – at work or outside of it. Her remark hits way too close to home. And not only because she's right about the "Blind Date Diaries".

"You know when Eli and I broke up, he said one of the problems with our relationship was my inability to have fun.

What he meant was, I was uptight. Because it turned out his version of fun was the sex-in-public-places kind." I give Melissa a wry look. "You know Rachel was fun."

"Stop. First of all, Jack Reese is not Eli Quinn. And second, you may think Jack is an ass, but at least he's forthright about it. He's not pretending he's a good guy, then turning around saying gotcha." Melissa points a finger at me, stopping just short of poking me in the shoulder.

"How ironic that the one point in his favor is that he's not masquerading as a decent human being." I roll my eyes.

"It doesn't mean he's not one. He could surprise you, you know. Besides, the Angeline Sinclair I know sure as hell can take whatever Jack Reese dishes out." Melissa gives me a death stare that lasts until we both giggle.

"Damn right." I run my hand through my hair, tugging the ponytail holder over my wrist as I do. "What if his version of a date is to take me to his place to pick up where we left off?"

"I don't see it." Melissa shakes her head. "For what it's worth, I think he's going to take you on a real date."

"Yeah." I nod, my words coming out slowly. "I kind of think so, too."

"Who knows? You might discover you actually like him."

"I've thought of that, and it seems unlikely." Then again, two weeks ago hooking up with him felt unlikely, too.

Chapter Eight

ANGELINE

6:05.

Jack is late. I'm perched on a chair in the lobby of *Pink* pretending to be fascinated by my phone. Partly to avoid the gaze of the temporary receptionist — a redhead today — and partly to give myself a distraction. It's either scan through Instagram or pace the lobby, and even though I'm dying to pace, it's too obvious.

I could have waited in my office and paced in peace, but there are enough people still here that I don't want to have to parade across the floor with Jack. Everyone knows tonight is date night and I half-suspect they're lying in wait to see how it goes. Or if he shows. If I had money to place a bet, I'd put the odds at forty percent and sinking.

I bite my lip, lipstick be damned, and swipe through to Twitter. I can at least catch up on whatever is outraging the internet today while I wait. As I scan my feed looking for something interesting enough to take my attention away from the clock at the top — 6:07 now — the door opens, bringing a blast of hot air with it.

My shoulders straighten, but my attention remains on my

phone, even though I'm no longer reading. I can't because holy cologne, Batman. I like a good aftershave as much as the next girl, but the wave of scent is strong. And a little bit...floral? I sniff the air as I look up to see Jack. And Victoria?

What. The. Hell?

I rise from my chair just as the temporary receptionist says, "Welcome to *Pink*. Can I help you?"

Neither Jack nor Victoria even look at her, although Victoria says, "We're fine, thank you." Then she turns to me and says, "I was in the neighborhood and thought I'd pop by, and look who I ran into?"

I offer a close-lipped smile because it feels like she was in the neighborhood to make sure this date really happened. That doesn't ease my nerves at all. "Imagine. Jack, nice of you to make it."

"I'm sorry I'm late," Jack says. He doesn't sound or look sorry. "But unfortunately, Mother, because of it, we have to leave rather immediately."

I've never heard Jack sound so formal, and it almost makes me smile. Then I look at him for the first time. He's shaved and wearing black trousers and a short-sleeved, blue-and-white stripe button down that makes his eyes a dark indigo blue. Piercing. Trained on me in a way that swallows my smile whole and makes my stomach lurch with...anticipation? Whatever it is, I'm glad I took Melissa's advice and upped my game tonight.

"Are you ready, Angeline?" Jack asks, taking a step closer and holding out his arm.

Since when did Jack have those sinewy muscles in his forearm? Probably always, but I haven't noticed them before, and noticing them now feels wrong. I can't take his arm. Can't. Won't. Instead I pick my purse up from the chair, clutching it in both hands, and nod. "Sure, let's go. Victoria, I'll see you Monday to go over the mock-ups for the print run?"

"Of course. I'll be here at ten," Victoria says. "Have fun, you two, and Jack, I'll see you for tea on Sunday at four."

She doesn't phrase it as a question and judging from the way Jack stiffens beside me, it's not an invitation as much as an order. He doesn't respond, just pulls the door and ushers me through it.

We don't speak on our way to the parking lot behind the office. I give my second-hand Honda a longing glance as I look for Jack's car. We took an Uber to his place the other night, so I have no idea what he drives. I envision a Porsche or maybe an old-style Corvette. I had an old boyfriend who had a Corvette once and, I'll tell you a secret, it's true what they say about sports cars compensating for something.

So color me surprised when Jack fishes the keys from his pocket and clicks them at a charcoal gray Jeep Wrangler, complete with roll bars and an open roof. "This is your car?" I ask.

"No, it's Chris's. I didn't think you'd appreciate the pick-up truck I use for work. It smells like turpentine." Jack nods towards the Jeep. "This roof closes, don't worry."

"I wasn't worried." My voice trails off as Jack opens the door for me, waiting until I slip into the passenger seat before pushing it closed. Okay, who is this guy and what has he done with the real Jack Reese? Because Jack Reese, gentleman, is as hard to wrap my head around as those muscles I keep noticing.

He gets into the passenger seat, turns the key, and the engine roars to life. He closes the roof, but not the windows, which I'm glad about, eighty-five-degree temperatures be damned. The Jeep already feels small and without fresh air I'd be two steps away from claustrophobic. In two quick turns he's out of the parking lot and onto Main Street, where he says, "We're running late – my fault, I know – but I'm going to need to make up time."

Then he floors it, passing the car in front, and barreling

towards the highway. Instinctively, I grab the oh-shit handle above the door, but I'm not scared. My dad has always been a fast driver, urged on by my brothers and me, and Jack's driving is fast, but careful and controlled. He doesn't speak as he merges onto the busy 495, weaving in and out of the Friday afternoon traffic. Not until we slow on the exit ramp does he turn to me and say, "You did better than I thought you would."

"Sorry to disappoint you. Were you expecting shrieking and white knuckles?" I roll my eyes.

"Not at all." Jack grins. "Demands and clenched fists are way more your style."

"You pay attention after all." I raise my eyebrows and manage to hold his gaze. No small feat when I'm noticing that his smile is genuine. And damn sexy. "So where are we going?"

"The Rochester Lyceum. How do you feel about chocolate?"

"Is that a real question?"

"Well, if you're allergic or something, then obviously we'll have to pivot, but otherwise we're going to make chocolate." Jack looks pleased with himself, but I'm not sure it's not for the use of the word pivot. "I've signed us up for a chocolate-making class at 6:30. Great idea, right?"

It is a great idea, especially as first dates go. I'd probably say that if Jack didn't go there first. So instead I say, "It will make a good story for the 'Blind Date Diaries'."

"Speaking of, let me ask you. Predate effort, five out of ten? Or did I warrant a six?" There's that cocky tone that sets my teeth on edge. And proof he saw the mock-up template. Thanks, Victoria.

"Four." In truth, at least a six. Seven, if you count Melissa insisting I wear more eye makeup. "What about you? Same?"

"I ironed, sweetheart. That's at least a five." Jack shoots me a grin that could be taken as self-deprecating if I ignore the way his eyes narrow like they did the other night.

"You ironed? Don't you mean your mother's staff ironed your shirt? I don't think that counts."

"My mother's staff?" Jack's laugh ricochets off the dashboard. "Let me assure you, they have been directed not to cater to me."

"A wise order, no doubt." I'm not sure I do a very good job of hiding my surprise. Jack ironed? For me? I mean, maybe it wasn't for me, but I've never seen him in a freshly pressed shirt before. Not even at Victoria's swanky garden party over Memorial Day weekend. The party was for *Pink* staff, so Jack wasn't formally invited, but he showed up anyway, wearing a wrinkled linen shirt, plaid shorts, and flipflops while the rest of us sweated it out in our Sunday best.

"Occasionally I can convince Jane, the housekeeper, to pass along some dinner party leftovers, but it's rare." Jack lets out an exaggerated sigh. "Then again, who really wants day-old salmon soufflé?"

"No one. That's disgusting." I make a face.

"Trust me, it's not as bad as the ham croquettes." It's Jack's turn to make a face. "They sound better, but they're the worst thing I've ever eaten. And, of course, Mother doesn't eat so telling her is futile."

I laugh because Jack's assessment of Victoria is unexpected and totally on point. "She doesn't eat, does she? Why is that?"

"Who knows?" Jack's smile fades. "You can never be too rich or too thin, right?"

I think you can. Especially the latter. But it's probably not a great idea to criticize my boss to her son. Instead, I say, "So if Jane's not hooking you up, you must have to cook for yourself. What's your specialty?"

Jack turns into the parking lot of the Rochester Lyceum, so his eyes are on the road as he says, "Trying to get to know me now? Have you had a change of heart I should know about, because if you have, I'm all ears."

My face flushes. That's exactly what I was doing, and I hate that it was such a transparent attempt almost as much as I hate Jack's smug tone. "Sorry. Didn't realize you'd object."

"Who said anything about me objecting?" Jack raises an eyebrow. "I just want to know if the rules have changed."

"What rules are those?"

"The ones where you assume you know everything there is to know about me and I let you." Jack's eyes hold a hint of a challenge.

"You let me?" I emphasize the word *let*.

"In this case, yes." Jack's lips curve up, but he doesn't quite smile. "Maybe it's easier for both of us to let you think I'm an asshole, you know?"

Quite frankly, I don't know. It's on the tip of my tongue to ask why he would do that, but then I eye up his ironed shirt again, and suddenly I'm not sure I want to ask after all.

Scratch that. I want to ask. But I'm not sure I want to know the answer.

Chapter Nine

JACK

I cracked open the door on the truth with Angeline and it made my balls sweat. That's a fucking first. We're following some blonde teenage girl down the hall through the Rochester Lyceum and I'm so nervous my balls are actually sweating. I keep waiting for Angeline to call me on what I said in the Jeep, but she's been quiet.

Funeral quiet.

Which makes my balls sweat more.

When we get to the kitchen and I gesture for Angeline to go first, she says, "Are you secretly chivalrous, too?"

"Not so secretly, sweetheart." I grin. "I took etiquette classes when I was twelve, you know."

"You did not." Angeline's eyes widen.

"Oh, I did. You have met my mother?" I put on a falsetto. "'Darling, you won't go far in life if you don't know how to use the right fork.'"

"That sounds like Victoria." Angeline laughs. "So, what happened?"

"To my manners?" Heat spreads up my back. Thank God I went heavy on the deodorant. "Nothing."

"So you meant what you said then? It's in your best interest for me to think you're an asshole?"

"I didn't say it's in my best interest, sweetheart. I said it's easier." This is the truest thing I've said this year, but I'm done with true confession time because standing in a kitchen class-room isn't exactly how I pictured this conversation going down. Especially with Miss Blue Hair in the next row over taking an avid interest in our conversation. "So, are we making chocolate or what?"

"Chocolate. Yes." Angeline blinks like she'd forgotten what we're doing here and looks around. "This is a pretty swanky set up."

She's right. There are three rows of counters with two stove tops each and imposing blocks of knives next to baskets of onions and garlic. I don't see anything that looks like it's required to use in chocolate-making, but then again what do I know? I take one of the knives out of the block and say, "I make a mean spaghetti sauce. Lots of hidden veg."

Judging by the way Angeline's mouth twists, she realizes immediately I'm going back to our conversation in the Jeep. I half-expect her to call me on it – because Angeline Sinclair isn't the type to let shit lie – but she doesn't. Instead she nods and says, "There's a lot to be said for vegetables, especially when they're hidden."

"What about you? Do you cook?"

"Not very well. I make a good garlic peppercorn sauce for steak, but only if someone else is cooking the steak."

Note to self: a barbecue date would not be out of the question.

"Lucky for you I'm a grill master."

Angeline laughs, and I'm not exaggerating when I say it's phenomenal. Because I'm pretty sure it's the first genuine moment we've ever had, including the one in my kitchen. It's probably a good thing I don't get to think too much about that because Leslie, the instructor, comes in, claps her hands, and says, "Welcome, everyone. Are we ready to make some chocolate?"

There are murmurs of assent and Leslie sends us all to wash our hands, which puts an end to any further conversation between Angeline and me. In fact, we don't get to talk about anything other than ingredients and measuring until after we've put our chocolate to cool in the refrigerator.

As I wash the pots, I ask, "So, the 'Blind Date Diaries'? Your idea or my mother's?"

"Is that a real question?" Angeline picks up a spoon to dry. "Your mother's."

"Why? It's not exactly on brand."

"I know, no pressure, right?" Angeline rolls her eyes a little. "It's a huge gamble for *Pink*. You weren't really given a choice to be my date, but we only had a few entries this week anyway. If we're going to get the readership and the advertising dollars behind this, everything about it needs to be good, possibly even great. People don't tune in to *The Bachelorette* in droves because she's having a terrible time. They tune in because she's having an amazing time on all of her dates and it's going to be that much harder for her to choose."

"You are not going to end this thing with a rose ceremony." I widen my eyes in mock horror.

Angeline laughs. "Um, no. I was thinking something along the lines of a second date?"

"Aim high, sweetheart." I grin. "So, you want to write up a piece titillating enough to capture the readers' imagination and make them believe you like me."

"Titillating. Yes. Exactly." She pauses, but not long enough for me to respond. "And make them believe you like me, of course."

"I like you more than you think." I hand her a pot, but don't let go.

"So you said." She doesn't meet my eyes.

"Is it that you genuinely don't believe me, or you don't want to?" I let go of the pot. She still doesn't look at me.

Also, my balls are sweating again. Traitors.

"I just don't understand –" Angeline starts and then stops, glancing over to Miss Blue Hair, who's leaning halfway over the counter towards us. "I'm sorry. Do you need something?"

"I was just thinking that you look awfully familiar and I had to ask. Do you go to yoga at the Studio over in Henrietta?" Her voice has a slight southern twang and reminds me of my grandmother. Normally, I'd soften at that, but not now.

Angeline, though, changes completely. Her back straightens. She flicks her hair and pastes on a smile as she says, "No yoga for me, unfortunately, although I keep meaning to give it a try. I'm the managing editor of *Pink*. Are you a reader?"

"Oh, my goodness, you are." Miss Blue Hair lowers her voice. "Are you on your blind date?"

Angeline nods and turns back to me. "This is Jack."

Miss Blue Hair gives me an appraising look and turns back to Angeline. "I can see why you picked him for your first date."

Angeline laughs. It's tinny and nothing like her real laugh earlier. "Oh, I didn't pick him. The readers pick my dates."

I know – I fucking know – she's working. If not overtly, then on some managing-editor-sales level. I've seen my mother do the same thing, flip the same switch. But her easy denial stings because it feels like she's saying, *I didn't pick him*. Period.

I tune out their conversation. Class will be over soon and then this farce of a date is over, too. At least I've managed to get my mother off my back – and her nose out of my business. So, yeah. Box checked. Sure, maybe I thought I could turn a fake date into something real, but I've learned a valuable lesson. Angeline doesn't see me as date material and thinking she could possibly see me as more makes me look - and feel - like a fool.

Chapter Ten

ANGELINE

I'm about one truffle away from murdering the woman with blue hair in this class. If she says how easy chocolate making is one more time, I might do it. I mean, sure, it's easier than I thought it would be, but it's not something I could do blindfolded. Or maybe I'm just wound extra tight because being here with Jack has been easier than I thought it would be, too.

He's taken this whole date thing seriously, measuring ingredients, stirring the butter and cream together, and even listening attentively when Leslie, the instructor, gave us a mini lecture on the history of chocolate before we put our truffles in the refrigerator.

I like you more than you think?

Hello, did I know you liked me at all? I'm still reeling a little from that one. If I were going to complain, it might be that he's been a little too earnest.

Which is ridiculous, because this version of Jack is so much easier to deal with than the one who goads me until I can't think straight. Never mind the sarcasm he serves up like gravy on a turkey dinner. But at least I know how to deal with that. This is uncharted territory.

When Leslie claps her hands and tells us all to get our trays out of the refrigerator, I raise my eyebrows at Jack. "What do you think? Do you think you curdled the cream?"

"Unlikely, sweetheart." Jack scowls, but just as quickly puts his date face back on. "Should we add any toppings? Nuts maybe?"

"You like nuts, do you?" I don't mean it *that* way. But damn if I don't expect him to react anyway.

"Leslie said macadamia nuts go well with chocolate because of their buttery texture." Jack's tone says everything his words don't. Something along the lines of *I'm not playing your juvenile game*, if I had to venture a guess. "Do you want to take a before and after photo for the magazine?"

"I should." I pull my phone out of the back pocket of my jeans. "Do you want to be in it?"

"Hell, no" He takes a step back for emphasis.

"It would be good publicity." I offer. "I saw Jack Reese Designs has an ad in this week's issue."

"Um, yeah." Jack nods and shuffles his feet for a second. When he glances back at me, he looks sheepish. "That was a Victoria Buchanan extra."

I furrow my brow because it takes me a minute to understand. But when I do, I get it loud and clear. "You mean you got an ad in exchange for coming out with me tonight? That's why you were so willing to do this?"

Saying the words leaves a taste in my mouth like I've just eaten a stack of burnt toast. Which is ridiculous. This isn't a real date. I know that.

"Nah. Victoria's pretty tight about giving me access to *Pink*. It's one thing for me to do some work in the office, it's another to put my custom woodwork on the pages of her precious magazine. I paid for it, but she didn't axe it, which was a nice change." Jack's voice is low so no one around us can hear. Which is good because I don't need my new best friend with the blue hair getting any more interested in our conversation than she already is.

"That's great. It's really good exposure for you." I flash a plastic smile and grab the tray of chocolates. "So, we're rolling these in nuts, right?"

"Ang..." Jack starts.

"It's cool, Jack. I'm impressed you were able to wrangle an ad out of her." My smile feels a little more real this time. "And at least now I know what my going rate is."

"Maybe you should have a rate card printed up?" Jack's voice drops and his eyebrows go up. "I can think of a few things to put on it."

"Can you now?" I let the flirtation slip into my tone. I know how to do this. Dealing with the thud in my stomach that Jack's admission creates? Not so much.

I manage to push it aside all through the rest of the class and through the cleaning up. Leslie's a stickler for washing up and I end up getting called back for forgetting a bowl. A fact Jack teases me about once we're back outside by the car. "Are you going to include the fact that the teacher made you stay after class in your article?"

"Don't be silly. You're only my first date and you were paid to be here. I need to reel in the other ones and telling them I'm a slob isn't going to do it." Oh my God. I hate how needy my voice sounds in my head, so I'm sure it comes out even worse.

Jack's smile fades. "Ang, I'm sorry. The ad thing..."

"Like I said, no worries. It was good business on your part." I make a show of glancing at my watch so I don't have to see the expression on Jack's face. "Hey, it's still early. You could probably fit in an actual date if you've planned properly."

"You were my actual date for the evening, but it's kind of

you to point that out." He frowns. "Do you have other plans I should know about?"

"No. Food and wine are on my to-do list, but that's not a plan as much as a necessity." And that was not me angling for an invitation. Well, almost definitely not.

"I'm probably going to regret this, but do you want to get something to eat?" Jack shoves his hand through his hair like he can't quite believe those words just came out of his mouth.

"Wow. There's an offer I can't refuse." I manage to bark out a laugh, but I don't think it hides the hurt in my expression. "'I'm probably going to regret this?' Really?"

"Dammit. That's not what I meant." Jack's eyes close and he looks as weary as I feel all of a sudden.

"That's what you said." I'm also pretty sure he meant it at least a little bit.

Further proof? Jack's eyes pop open and he says, "You know what? It's fine. I'll take you back to your car and we'll call it a night."

"No need. I live off Park Ave. You can drop me off and I'll get my car in the morning." Pittsford is at least fifteen minutes further and I'm dying a slow death inside already. Fifteen more minutes might kill me. Or make me cry.

"I'm not going to just drop you off. I can only imagine what you'll say about that in your diary entry. What did you call it in your mock-up? The deal-breaker moment?" Jack's voice has that tone again.

"We both know what the deal-breaker moment was. And it won't be you dropping me off at Sergio's so I can get a couple slices."

"You know damn well I didn't mean it that way. Especially if you listened to anything else I've said tonight." He spins on his heel and strides over to the driver's side. In one fluid motion, he clicks his seatbelt, puts the car into gear, and says. "Are you going to close your door, or do I need to come around and do it for you?"

I yank the door closed with a resounding thud and then I make myself hold his gaze when I say, "I did listen to what you said, Jack. But you say one thing, then contradict it with another, which makes me think maybe you don't mean any of it."

Jack pauses with his hand on the gear shift. "I thought tonight could be different. My bad."

He's not blaming me, but it feels like he is. "Different than what?"

Jack opens his mouth and it looks like he's going to answer. Then he shuts it and shakes his head. When he opens his mouth again, he says, "I don't know. Just different."

He sounds dejected.

I shrug a little and say, "Yeah, well."

And that's all I say because I can't help noticing. I sound dejected, too.

Chapter Eleven

ANGELINE

*J*ack and I don't speak for the ten minutes it takes to drive to Park Avenue until he pulls into an empty parking space and turns the engine off. The fact that he found a parking space on Park Ave on a Friday night is more proof that he and I have nothing in common because I've lived here my entire life and it's never occurred to me to even try to park on Park Ave on the weekend. Although it begs the question why he's parking at all.

"What are you doing?" I ask.

"Walking you home," Jack says.

"I don't want you to walk me home." The minute he finds out I live with my father, he'll mock me forever. "There are tons of people around."

"Sorry, sweetheart. I insist." Jack takes the key out of the ignition. "But we can get pizza on the way if you want."

"What if I don't want you to know where I live? There's a reason you picked me up from work." I don't want him to know where I live, but my reasoning is flimsy and I know it.

So does Jack. "The reason I picked you up at work is

because that's where you were going to be and we had a schedule to keep. I doubt I could have convinced you to leave early. As for me knowing where you live, do you really think I couldn't find out your address in thirty seconds or less if I wanted to?"

Another point to Jack. Google still shows my Upper West Side address, but he doesn't need Google when he's got Victoria, does he? "Which obviously you wouldn't do because that would make you more creepy, rather than less."

"I didn't say I wanted to. I just said I could."

"A fine distinction. But whatever. I'd rather go than argue with you." At this point, I'd rather stick needles in my eyes than continue to argue with him.

"Fine." Jack opens his car door and hops out of the Jeep.

It takes me three seconds to follow. Three seconds where I think about giving in and admitting defeat. I'm tired and hungry and I can't maintain this level of tension much longer without either losing my cool or bursting into tears. My sense of self-preservation tells me screaming or crying will lead to Jack pitying me for the rest of my days. And possibly telling Victoria I'm unhinged. Neither option is appealing, so I take a deep breath as I exit the Jeep and plant my feet on the sidewalk. I make myself look Jack in the eye and say, "I don't want to do this."

"I said I was walking you home and I –"

"I mean I don't want to argue with you. I'm done. You win. Whatever." My voice drops and, damn, if it doesn't waver a little.

Which, of course, Jack hears. He comes closer and peers down at me. "Hey. What is it? What's wrong?"

"I don't want to argue with you anymore, that's all." And there were moments when tonight was fun. Where I thought he liked me. And I let myself like him. I'll never say any of that out loud, of course, so I weakly add, "Please."

Jack studies me for another few second. It feels like he's staring into my soul, which makes me squirm. Because my hidden depths are just that – hidden – and I don't want Jack Reese trying to unearth them somehow. After a long minute he nods. "I'm sorry. Let me buy you a pizza to make it up to you?"

He holds his arm out for me to take his elbow, and because it feels like a white flag gesture, I take it. We make our way arm-in-arm down Park Avenue, which might be the weirdest part of this evening so far, but it's better than being mad. Or sad. We don't speak, but this time our silence feels less fraught and my shoulders have just about dropped back to where they belong when Jack tenses beside me and whispers, "Shit."

My eyes widen in a question, but I don't get to ask before a leggy redhead wearing a tulle skirt and a black leather biker vest steps out of Monroe's Bar and Grill and flashes a wide smile at Jack. She's edgy and cool and looks like a funky ballerina. "Well, well, well. Look who it is. Jack Reese, I haven't seen you in a month of Sundays."

"Katarina. It's good to see you." I don't know Jack very well, but I don't hear much sincerity there.

Apparently neither does Katarina because she pouts and says, "Oh, Jack. Surely you can do better than that for your almost-wife."

My gaze flies to her hand, but I don't see a ring. *Almost-wife* doesn't equal fiancée, but it's not a casual label either. I'm still fixated on Katarina's word choice when Jack says, "That was a long time ago."

Katarina turns to me, glancing at my hand in the crook of Jack's arm. "Did Jack tell you he was engaged back in the day?"

No, he one hundred percent did not. But judging by the way he's tensed up beside me, saying that is only going to make things worse. So I shrug and smile a little. "Of course. But we all have a skeleton or two in our closet, right?"

"Well, right." Katarina laughs. I half-expect her to twirl

because her skirt makes her seem like the twirling type. She doesn't, though, and says, "So, how did you two meet?"

I'm fairly sure telling Katarina the real story would be a terrible idea and she doesn't really strike me as a *Pink* reader. Which means she might not find out the truth. Then again, I'm not the best judge of character, and for all I know she's *Pink*'s biggest fan. Which calls for a version of the truth. "We met on a blind date, believe it or not, and we've been together ever since."

Katarina raises both eyebrows this time. "A blind date? I've never known Jack to go on a blind date in my life."

"Well, it just takes one." I aim a smile at Jack. "Right, sweetheart?"

"That, it does." Jack's grin is genuine, and I'm still thinking about that dimple in his cheek when he says to Katarina, "We're going to get some food, but it was great running into you."

"Yeah. It was really great. Enjoy..." Katarina waves her hand like she's brushing away a gnat. "You know, everything. And great to meet you? I don't think I caught your name?"

"No, I don't think you did," Jack says. "See you around, Kat."

He steps forward, tugging me along as Katarina gapes after us. I feel the giggle building in my chest, so I don't dare look at Jack until we turn into Sergio's on the next block. Where my laugh rings out across the small waiting area, mingling with his as we join the back of the line.

"You were kind of incredible back there," Jack says, his grin wide.

Again.

Still.

It's been a long time since a guy has looked at me the way Jack's looking at me now. And I can't help grinning in reply. "I only told the truth."

"I know. Which is what makes it even more brilliant." Jack laughs, but it fades into a sigh. "I am sorry about that. Kat and I..."

I hold up my hand. "It's fine. You don't have to explain."

"I broke things off with her. I wasn't ready and she wasn't the right person for me. There were ten different reasons, but I wasn't the good guy in that scenario. Just so you know." Jack's expression isn't one I've ever seen from him before, but I recognize it. He owns the truth behind that story, whatever it is.

Which is the only reason I can think of that the next words come out of my mouth. "My fiancé cheated on me with someone named Rachel. The day I moved out, I cut the crotch out of all of his boxer briefs."

Jack lets out a low laugh. "Sounds to me like he deserved it."

"You think?" I laugh, too.

"Kat took my favorite hoodie and set it on fire." Jack laughs again, but this time it's deeper. Richer. "The only saving grace was that I wasn't wearing it at the time."

"If I could've gotten the scissors near Eli when he was dressed, it would have been a whole different thing." I try to roll my eyes but I'm trying harder not to laugh.

"I still don't feel sorry for Eli." Jack chuckles.

"Who'd have thought that would be something we'd have in common?" I laugh for real this time.

"Oh, I don't know. We both like chocolate with nuts, and I've got you pegged for a veggie-only pizza." Jack says as we shuffle towards the front of the line.

"I love a veggie pizza, but I can live with extra cheese if you want pepperoni or something. Melissa has a thing about vegetables touching her meatlovers half, so if we're sharing, I just get extra cheese." A point I used to argue about but don't anymore because Melissa's such a baby about it – and she makes up for it by splitting an order of chicken with garlic sauce if we order from Hong Kong Chinese. A choice I know offends her because her go-to dish is beef with broccoli every time.

"Today's your lucky day because veggie pizza is my favorite," says Jack, picking up the menu from the counter.

"Do you want to share?" Two minutes ago, I was planning on a couple slices to go – to be enjoyed with a glass of Cabernet on the couch watching Netflix. Alone. Considering Sergio's has only a handful of tables in the back, the chance of us snagging one on a Friday night is slim. Which means the only way Jack and I are sharing a pizza is by sitting on the couch at my dad's, but I'm not sure the truce we've declared is strong enough to survive that.

Not that my dad is likely to even be home – he's got a better social life than I do – but on the off chance he is? Horrifying. Mortifying. Every other possible *-fying* you can think of.

Jack seems to have the same realization, without even knowing about my dad. "If we order a full pie and have them split it, it's cheaper than ordering slices, and it tastes better because it's made fresh."

That makes sense, and even though it doesn't solve the where-to-eat problem, I nod and dig in my bag for my wallet because this feels like the kind of situation where I should insist on paying. "That's great. Let me get this because you treated me to the chocolate-making class."

"No." Jack puts his hand on my arm. "You rescued me from my ex. I owe you a lot more than a pizza."

I glance down at Jack's hand. His grip is loose on my arm, but I feel it like a weight. A warm, strong, callused weight, which is why my reply has nothing to do with paying for pizza when I ask, "How long have you been in the carpentry business?"

"Why? Worried I can't afford a pizza, sweetheart?" Jack's tone is flat and my eyes fly up as he drops his hand. He's got that smirk I'm used to seeing and his eyes hold none of the softness I didn't even realize was there five minutes ago.

Instinct almost makes me snap back at him, but I just shake my head. "Of course not. I was just curious, that's all." I force a smile. "By all means, don't tell me if it means you'll have to kill me because I have an article to write this weekend."

Jack's eyes narrow and I think for a second he's going to brush me off with another smart remark, until he says, "Six years. I had an office job for a couple years after college and did carpentry on the side. But it got to the point where I was either going to move up the corporate ladder or go full out with my own thing, so I took the risk. Mostly I do custom work, like the bookshelves I'm doing for *Pink*, entertainment consoles, and wardrobes, but I also build furniture. I've got a studio in East Rochester where I do most of my restorations and smaller pieces. Sometimes I do odd jobs to pay the bills, like when I saw you at Oh My Bagel a few days ago."

"Do you like it?"

"Being my own boss suits me." Jack grins. "I'm not a great employee."

"Will you be offended if I say I can totally see that?"

"Not even a little offended." Jack laughs and it's a genuine one that floods my chest with warmth. "So, are we ordering or what?"

I do the whole smile eye-roll thing, which I suddenly feel is my default mode, and say, "Of course. Go ahead. As long as you don't try to sneak pepperoni onto my half."

"Don't worry, sweetheart. You can trust me." Jack says this as he saunters up to the counter.

As I watch him walk away, two thoughts vie for space in my head. The first— Jack Reese has a nice ass – and the second – maybe I could trust him – are nothing compared to the one that pops up unbidden as he chuckles about something with the guy behind the counter.

Maybe I could like him, too.

Chapter Twelve

THE "BLIND DATE DIARIES"

*P*ink Ladies – It's Tuesday and you know what that means! Blind date recap time.

Pre-date effort: *7 out of 10 – Leaving straight from work is tricky, right?*

Nerves: *1 out of 10 – On the other hand, leaving straight from work has its advantages.*

Date location: *10 out of 10 – A chocolate-making class at the Rochester Lyceum. Highly recommend – for a first date or a group of friends.*

First impression: *6 out of 10 – Being almost ten minutes late isn't a great way to start any date, especially a blind date.*

HOWEVER. Chocolate-making is a great way to break the ice. There's a task to focus on – and a built-in topic of conversation – plus, you can observe how well your date follows instructions and works as a team. Admittedly, I wasn't looking at him this way until after the fact, but I'd give him a 10 out of 10 on both counts. Trust me, no one is more shocked than I am about that. Not to say there wasn't a red flag moment or two...

Red flag #1: *The phrase 'I'm probably going to regret this'* *followed immediately by an invitation to dinner? Cue me shaking my head and muttering.*

Blind date rule #1: *Sticking to the original parameters of the date is fine. There's no need to extend drinks into dinner or dinner into dessert unless you think you kinda', sorta' want to know if he chews with his mouth open (he doesn't) or prefers cake vs pie (Cake all the way. Chocolate cake. In case you were wondering.)*

Red flag #2: *Jalapenos on pizza. Some warning would have been nice.*

Blind date rule #2: *Not everyone loves hot peppers. Yours truly included.*

Deal breaker moment: *Some close calls, but ultimately...none.*
Possibility of second date: *Um...?*

Chapter Thirteen

ANGELINE

"Oh my God. You had a great time." Melissa looks up from the paper in her hand, her eyes wide.

"I did. It was weird, but good." I rake my fingers through my hair. "I don't know. It wasn't what I expected."

Especially dinner – which we ended up eating sat on a bench in front of Sergio's people-watching – followed by coffee and cake at That Cake Place, which gets zero points for its name and all the points for its molten chocolate cake.

"Did you kiss him?" Melissa asks, wriggling her eyebrows.

I shake my head. "No. It wasn't like that."

But it wasn't not like that either. Eating pizza together was pure happenstance. Jack asked if I minded sitting down on the bench so he could have a slice because he was starving, and we ended up sitting there and talking, eating the whole thing. Dessert was more deliberate, which dawned on both of us as we approached the end of my street. I drew the line at him walking me to my dad's front door, but the end of the street was doable.

"So, what was it like?" asks Melissa.

I motion for her to close my office door. She does and leans forward in the chair in front of my desk, but I lower my voice anyway. "Honestly, it was awkward at the end. Neither of us really knew what to do and I ended up shaking his hand."

My cheeks flush at the memory and heat up another five degrees when Melissa lets out a whoop of laughter. "You shook his hand?"

"Ssshhh. I know." I drop my head in my hands. "I am such a dork."

"What did he do?" Melissa has the decency to bite her lip to try to keep from laughing, but a giggle escapes.

"He shook my hand and then leaned over and kind of kissed my cheek." More like brushed my cheek with his lips because I was surprised and stepped back as he leaned in.

Like I said. Awk. Ward.

"Did you want to kiss him?"

"Yes? Maybe?" I make a face, but my heart's not in it.

"You already hooked up with him, so why so shy all of a sudden?" Melissa gives me that piercing stare of hers.

Because when I kissed him before it was driven by the loose, anxious kind of desire that fuels bad decisions. If I'd kissed him on Friday night, the desire would have been for Jack alone. Eli was the last person I kissed because I liked him and look how that turned out.

"He's still Victoria's son." I hold up my hand before she can speak. "But even if he wasn't, I'm not looking to get involved with anyone right now."

"Okay. First of all, Victoria was the one who set this whole thing up. Second, being genuinely not ready is one thing. Saying you're not ready because you're scared of developing feelings for someone again is another." Melissa waits for me to disagree, but I can't because I spent too much time this weekend thinking the same thing. "Have you heard from him since Friday?"

I nod. "We've texted a little."

"Let's see." Melissa holds out her hand for my phone.

"Sorry, no. My eyes only." It's not that Jack and I even said anything very personal. I just don't want Melissa to analyze our exchange and make me see it in a different light, because the Jack texting me isn't the Jack I thought I knew.

"Ooh la la. Sexting already, are we?"

"Well, I always have been better expressing myself with words than in actions." I point to the galley pages in her hand. "Do you think that's okay? Not only is Jack going to read it, but his mother is as well."

Melissa scans the page again and nods. "Have you two already talked about a second date?"

"I don't know. Sort of?" Over cake, we talked about antiques and Jack said he's restoring a sideboard from the 1920s, complete with Jacobean carving. When I ooh'd and ahh'd, he invited me to stop by his studio after work one night and then suggested a meal afterwards, but we didn't nail down specifics.

"You know leaving the probability of a second date open here is the equivalent of you asking him out, right? Maybe not directly, but it could be construed that way."

"Sure, but isn't this whole thing supposed to be titillating enough to keep people coming back week after week? What better way to achieve that than to keep them guessing?"

"Great point." Melissa grins. "Or is it that you know Jack's ego is going to demand he respond? I mean, can't you hear him now? 'So, you think the possibility of a second date is high, do you, sweetheart?'"

That is exactly what I hear. And it makes me smile, although I manage to keep a mostly straight face with Melissa. "We'll see. But the other part of this is making sure we generate enough interest for people to nominate next week's date and, as you said, coming across as positive is paramount."

Melissa doesn't get to respond because at that minute my office door flies open and Victoria enters in a cloud of perfume, pages in hand. "Angeline, I've read your piece and I like it. I don't love it, but I like it."

"Okay. What's wrong?" My tone is wary.

"There aren't any juicy details. I want to feel like I was there. It's the personal story that's going to draw readers in." Victoria waves the pages in her hand. "If you're calling it a diary, write a damn diary."

"I tried, but then it felt like too much detail. We went here. We did this. We did that." I shake my head. "Readers will lose interest."

"They will if you write it like that." Victoria's tone turns exasperated. "They want to know how you felt. This tells me nothing about how you felt, except that I think you must have enjoyed yourself because you're angling for a second date. But I see no evidence of enjoyment in this piece. You could have been out with your gynecologist for all I know."

That's because I didn't write about the part I enjoyed the most. I let out a sigh. "So what do you want me to do?"

"Rewrite it. You can do better and I expect it." Victoria holds out the pages for me to take and when I do take them — reluctantly — she says, "I'll be back in an hour."

I want to protest. Writing this yesterday took me two hours and I had a glass of wine to help me along. But I know Victoria won't budge, so I simply nod and watch her leave. Melissa follows, but turns with her hand on the doorknob saying, "Good luck. You've got this."

I shoot her a grateful smile and sink down into my desk chair as she closes the door. I open the "Blind Date Diaries" template and stare at the pink logo for a full minute before putting my fingers on the keyboard. The words come more readily than I thought they would, but telling the truth means nothing about this piece is going to be easy — especially the way it makes me feel.

Chapter Fourteen

JACK

*C*hris stops by my wood shop at 10:30 on Tuesday morning with a sandwich and a copy of *Pink* in hand. I take the foil-wrapped packet from his hand. "Special delivery? To what do I owe the honor?"

"I snagged a magazine for you." Chris holds out the copy of *Pink,* but I don't take it. "I thought you'd want to see the write up."

"Thanks for this, man. I owe you." I put the sandwich down on top of my workbench and unwrap it because I'm starving. I've been here since seven and have downed at least that many cups of coffee. I take a bite of the sandwich – hot ham and swiss with honey mustard on a sesame bagel – and let out a groan of pleasure. "Shit, this is good."

"Another sandwich of the day finds a fan. I'm going to call it My Funny Ham Melt Tine." Chris smiles and holds out the magazine again. "You want this?"

Yes.

No.

Maybe.

I settle for shaking my head and taking another bite of my

sandwich. I don't know why I don't want to read the article. Or maybe I just don't want to read it in front of Chris? I knew today was the day Angeline's write up would come out and I intend to read it. But I was planning on later. With a beer in hand, not a bagel sandwich.

I swallow and say, "Did you read it?"

Chris nods. "It's good."

His tone is neutral so I can't tell if he means the write up is genuinely good or it's well-written-but-she-slated-you good. I raise an eyebrow. "Give me a little more than that, dude."

Chris looks like he's trying not to smile. And failing. "She doesn't kiss and tell, if that makes a difference."

That's because there was no kiss to tell about, a moment I've kicked myself for more than once. I nod. "Good to know. Anything else?"

This time Chris's smile is wide. "I think she's into you."

I raise an eyebrow that's way more cynical than I feel when I say, "Yeah, I think you're reading it wrong. Angeline Sinclair borderline hates me."

Or at least she did before Friday night.

"Doesn't read that way to me." Chris shrugs. "Anyway, I've got to get back to the shop for the lunch rush."

"Sure. Did you need something, or did you come all the way over here to bring me this?" I furrow my brow and eye the half-eaten sandwich in my hand.

"I came all the way over here to bring you this." Chris holds *Pink* out to me and this time I take it. "And I needed to grab more baby spinach from Wegman's."

"What happened to the classic turkey with lettuce, tomato, and mayonnaise?"

"The health nuts like to sub spinach for iceberg. Makes them feel virtuous." Chris grins. "Happy reading. If you want to take Angeline a sandwich as a thank you for making you look good, her current favorite is a Brie My Baby."

A thank you for making me look good? My eyes dart to the magazine. "Do I even want to know what that is?"

"Melted brie with sliced apples and arugula on a sesame bagel. Turkey optional."

"Sounds disgusting, so I think I'll pass."

Chris's expression turns serious. "You should see her, though. You know that, right?"

"You know this wasn't my first date ever, right?" I roll my eyes.

"Okay, message received. But don't forget Brie My Baby. Or maybe an Avo You, Babe. Smashed avocado on a jalapeno bagel." Chris takes a step backwards. "You need more suggestions, I've got a million of them."

"Thanks, dude. I'll keep that in mind." I take another bite of my sandwich as Chris waves and turns towards the door.

I wait until he's shut the creaky door behind him before picking up the magazine. The cover is an explosion of pink, which, despite the name of the magazine, isn't normally the case. There's a silhouette of a man with the words the "Blind Date Diaries" across the torso in a swirly font. There are a few other teasers for articles inside the magazine, but the blind dating feature is obviously the focus.

I tap my foot as I flip through the pages searching for more pink. I assume it will be the center spread, but I'm not sure. They may have decided to save that for the nominations for next week's date.

Thinking that makes my foot tap faster and I flip until I catch the same swirly font on a right-facing page. I take a deep breath, look down, and start to read.

*T*he "Blind Date Diaries" – *Date Number Two Has A Lot to Live Up To*

You know how when you meet someone, you can't help forming an opinion of them? Normally, that opinion is formed within the first five minutes. For better or worse. And it's not like it can't change, but it's hard. Especially if that person reinforces your opinion of them when you meet again. And again. And again.

So imagine my surprise when, Jack, my first blind date – who, full disclosure, was not so blind because we'd met before – turned out to be completely different than I was expecting. In the best possible ways.

I let out a long breath and let my eyes close for a few seconds as my shoulders sink from where they've been hunched up by my ears. I try – and fail – to ignore the refrain in my head that's saying *holy shit, I have a chance* as I scan the rest of the article. It includes the expected pitch for the Rochester Lyceum and a sly dig at Miss Blue Hair until I get to the last paragraph.

I'm the first person to admit I was approaching this date with the same trepidation that most people feel when they see spiders in the shower. Times ten. To go out on a (relatively) blind date with someone I'd already put firmly in the no column and to have him turn into an oh-aren't-you-quite-nice by the end of a great evening was completely unexpected. And wonderful. I was on a serious high all weekend and am looking forward to seeing how Blind Date Number Two turns out. Oh, and Jack, if you're reading this (because I think you are, even if you won't admit it) thank you for a lovely date. And for the pizza. If you want to grab a slice sometime, next one's on me.

I'm grinning when I finish reading because I can hear Angeline's voice in my head saying those words in that slightly sarcastic tone she has. Chris was right. She made me look good, or, if not me, at least our date.

It was good. Really good. A little bit weird at the end because, even though we had that night in my kitchen, Angeline was sending out major not-sure-we're-at-the-kissing-stage-yet vibes. But before that? A ten out of ten.

Maybe Chris is right. I should bring her a sandwich. Or something. It would be cool to see her. Hear her laugh. I think about bringing her a few slices of pizza, but I'd want to get Sergio's and I don't have time to go all the way down to Park Avenue today. As it is, I've got to be on a job in Victor by one o'clock – a subcontract job fitting a wardrobe in a master bathroom. Not my usual thing, but it's the only woodworking part in a major bathroom renovation and I've worked with the general contractor before.

Oh My Bagel, it is. I glance at my watch as I take the last bite of my almost-forgotten sandwich. It's early for lunch, but if I leave here at noon, I can swing by and see Angeline on my way to Victor. I'll think about what to say once I get there, but for now I text Chris: *Can you have a Brie My Baby ready for me to pick up around noon?*

Chris's reply is immediate: *Will do. Glad you're following my advice.*

I grab my keys and don't bother to respond, but I can't deny it. I'm glad I'm following Chris's advice too. Even if it suddenly means the next hour is going to drag.

Chapter Fifteen

ANGELINE

I haven't let myself look at the finished piece in the magazine. Hell, I didn't even let myself reread my diary entry once I finished writing it yesterday. I handed it to Victoria and watched her face as she read it. She smiled her Botox smile when she finished, said, "That's more like it," and called Patrick to take over, so it was out of my hands.

If only it was out of my head as well. I know the magazine is out because I heard Mike from sales yelling about one of the temps hired to hand out free copies but was throwing up in the bathroom instead. Was that the impression we were going for?

To be fair, he had a point and I stand up from my desk chair, determined to find Mike to see how the temps turned out in the end. They were my idea, and only fell under Mike's jurisdiction because distribution is tied to sales. I'm halfway across the floor when I see Mike crossing through editorial, heading straight for me.

I wait because I can't get a read on him from this far away and if he's upset, I'd rather be able to close my office door to keep it contained. I've had a few disagreements with Mike in the eight months I've been here and, although I don't relish another one, it is a distraction from what's really on my mind. I haven't been able to get...

"I saw Jack Reese outside when I pulled up. He asked me to tell you he'd be stopping by in a few minutes," Mike says by way of greeting. It takes me a second to catch up with his actual words because my mind stuttered on the Jack Reese part, wondering if Mike had somehow turned into a mind reader.

"Uh, did he? Did he say why?" My voice feels strained and I hope Mike doesn't notice. I assume Jack read the article. But seeing him face-to-face on the heels of that? Different thing.

"Nope." Mike thrusts his hands into the pockets of his khaki pants and, not for the first time, I see the high school football player in his broad hulking form. According to my brother, Will, Mike was a football legend at some school down-state, recruited heavily for Division One college football, and destined for an NFL career until he tore his ACL playing tennis with his girlfriend the spring of his senior year. He had surgery and made a full recovery, but never played football again, which made a lot of people wonder — including Will — if he maybe never wanted to play at that level in the first place. It all seemed a bit conspiracy theory to me, but Mike seems perfectly happy selling advertising for a small local magazine and coaching his kids' soccer team on the weekends with nary a football in sight.

"Okay, well, we'll see." I straighten and put on a smile. "So, how did it go this morning?"

"Good, good. A little slow at first, but we ended up giving all the magazines away. I stuck around for a little while afterwards and noticed a fair number of people reading." Mike grins. "I even heard a couple people saying they were going to check out the Rochester Lyceum, and I've got a call in to them for a meet-ing. Hopefully they'll be flooded with inquiries by the time we meet and the ads will sell themselves."

"It was a great place. I'd recommend it if you and Lisa are looking for something different to do some time." I can't imagine Mike in a chocolate-making class, but then again, I couldn't imagine Jack either before we went. "That Cake Place would also be a great potential advertiser."

Mike nods. "Already on my radar. Any idea where you're going this Friday?"

"No. The voting on my potential date isn't live until tomorrow." My stomach sinks a little. I scanned through some of the nominations from last week and they were...fine. There were even one or two who I could see having a nice time with. Probably. Maybe not as nice a time as I ended up having with Jack, but that wasn't a true blind date either.

"Are we cooking the books this time?" Mike asks.

I shake my head. "This one is truly blind."

"So you'll be meeting the guy there? Maybe let me know so I can get in touch, build some momentum?"

My stomach sinks even further. The last thing I want is to build momentum for my date before I even have it, but then the whole point of this is to save the print edition. Which means increasing advertising dollars. Which means doing exactly what Mike's asking. I nod and say, "Sure. I should know by Thursday night. Once the guy is notified, he has until noon to get in touch with me or else we pick someone else."

"Right. And if both guys end up with cold feet, you go out with Reese again?"

"Um, I don't think so. Jack didn't really sign up for more than one date."

"I wouldn't be too sure about that." Mike's grin widens. "If you wrote about me the way you wrote about him in that piece, I'd be making sure there was a second date."

Oh God. My heart lurches. "What do you mean?"

"It came across like you like him. That's all." Mike's grin fades and he turns serious. "It's not a bad thing, Ang, and damn smart writing to get readers invested. It's like Melissa said when you pitched this idea. There's a reason those reality TV shows are so popular year after year. People eat this kind of thing up, especially if they think there might be real feelings involved."

I have two choices here and both make me feel twitchy. I can be honest with Mike and tell him I don't know how I feel, except that Jack Reese surprised me and I liked it. Or I can go with the out he gave me. It's a no-brainer because if I'm not going to level with my best friend, I'm certainly not going to confess my confusion to a colleague.

"I'm glad it worked because you're right, it's all about getting readers invested in this series. If they think I really like Jack, they're going to be all the more interested in date number two. I could probably even spin it like I'm torn between Jack and another guy like they do on *The Bachelorette*. There's a lot of potential there." My gaze is focused on Mike and with his bulk filling my doorway, I can't see anything behind him.

But I can hear just fine when Jack's voice says, "Always glad to be of service, sweetheart."

Crap. My heart plummets faster than a penny off the Empire State Building.

Mike moves out of the way to allow Jack to enter my office, sticking his hand out for a handshake. Jack takes it and does the whole guy nod thing, but his eyes are on me the whole time.

I can tell from his stance and the way his eyes gleam that he's annoyed. It makes me stand up straighter and press the heels of my hands into my hips. Classic battle stance, if I were going to have to battle.

Which is as ridiculous as Jack being mad in the first place. A few slices of pizza and a handful of texts don't mean we have a relationship. The tiny voice in my head telling me I owe Jack an apology disagrees, but I push it aside.

Mike clears his throat. "Well, okay. I just wanted to check in with you. Let me know where you're going on Friday?"

I nod and Mike shuffles out, pulling the door behind him so

it's almost closed, but not quite. Jack keeps his voice low when he says, "Your piece was good."

I widen my eyes in surprise because Jack did not – and does not – look like he's here to compliment me. "Thank you."

"Making readers believe you're emotionally invested is smart. If I were reading it blind, I'd believe you had a good time."

"I did have a good time, Jack." My voice comes out softer than I intend, but I'm afraid if I speak any louder it will sound nervous because that's how I feel, waiting for Jack to twist the knife of my words back at me.

"If you need me to pretend-fight over you, let me know. I'm always up for a bit of swagger and God knows I'm good at it, right?"

And there it is. Although instead of feeling relieved, it makes me feel horrible. "Dammit, Jack, stop it. You know –"

"I know what you wrote. I know what you said. And now I know what you meant." Jack turns and pulls the door open. "Like I said, sweetheart, happy to be of service. Have a nice day."

He ambles out like he doesn't have a care in the world, and I'm torn between watching him go and calling him back to explain. The only thing that stops me is the very real question – explain what?

I didn't mean what I said. I'm wary. I don't trust my own judgement.

Since I can't make myself say any of those things, I turn back to my desk and open my laptop, clicking on my email and scanning my inbox. It's the usual nonsense, except there's an email from Erin with the link to the profiles of nominations so far for this week's date. My stomach roils as I hover over the link and I squeeze my eyes shut. Then I open them and click the link like the adult I am trying to save her damn job.

Chapter Sixteen

ANGELINE

s I slow my little Honda to pull into Dad's driveway on Wednesday night, my head pounds and my eyes hurt. All I want to do is kick off my heels, take off my bra, and lay in my dark room until I feel well enough to dig through the freezer for some ice cream. Then I want to bring said ice cream back to bed and watch something mindless on Netflix.

Or think of a viable Plan B, because not only is Dad's car here, but Will's Tahoe and Theo's Camry are too – meaning there's a full house of Sinclair men tonight. I turn the engine off and sink back against my seat.

I love my brothers. I do. My Dad is amazing – and not only because he let me move back in with him when I fled Manhattan. My Mom died of a sudden heart attack ten years ago when I was a sophomore in college and, sure, he was reeling at first, but he's built himself a life now. Between work, a little fishing, and a lot of golf, he's got a better social life than Theo or me, for sure – and that doesn't even count the weekend barbecues and Wing Wednesdays that seem to pop up all the time. Will's probably got Dad beat in the socializing department, but I always say it's because his personal training clients invite him along to keep them honest, not for the pleasure of his company.

Mean, but you haven't met Will.

Maybe I can text Melissa and see if she wants to grab a drink? Even as I think it, I dismiss that notion. She'll want to talk about my potential dates or Jack, and I don't have the heart for that tonight. It's bad enough I had to review all the entries with Erin earlier. She wanted to weigh in on this week's date, and her preference skews towards the Jack Reese end of the spectrum – lots of brawn, not a lot of brains.

I meet my gaze in the rearview mirror and even my eyebrows reprimand me. That's not fair. I've done a bit of internet sleuthing and Jack's business is small but growing steadily. You don't succeed as an independent business – even in a city like Rochester – without tenacity and business savvy. Clearly Jack has both. He also has a good amount of talent. My digging unearthed his website too, where some of his custom work is listed for sale, and it's impressive – all clean lines and unexpected details. He has a dining room table for sale that Manhattan me would have convinced Eli to snap up in a New York minute, even at the four-thousand-dollar price tag.

I make a face at myself in the mirror. Rochester me doesn't have four thousand dollars, never mind the need for a dining room table, so there's no point thinking about it or the man who crafted it. Whom I've picked up my phone to text a thousand times since yesterday. The thing that stops me is what would I say? I'm sorry? Jack wouldn't let me apologize. Or if he would, he wouldn't let me do it in a way that assuages my guilty conscience. Although that's not his job, is it?

I hit the heel of my hand against my steering wheel in frustration, then force myself out of my car and up the front steps of my dad's house. Nothing puts me off men more than a night with my brothers and maybe by the time I'm done with them I won't give Jack a second thought. Especially if they're eating chicken wings. Which, judging by the smell that greets me as I walk into the kitchen, they totally are and have been for a while now.

"Ang!" Will's voice rings out first. "One of my clients mentioned your blind date thing. I think he's going to apply, and let me be the first to say, you should not go out with him."

I laugh and move towards the table strewn with boxes of buffalo wings and plastic cups of bleu cheese. "Why? What's wrong with him?"

"He thinks a lot of himself with no good reason." Will takes a bite of a stick of celery. Yes, my ultra-fit brother indulges in chicken wings, but only one or two max. Melissa says Will is good-looking – wavy brown hair, bright blue eyes, and a lean, muscular frame – and, objectively, I see it. But I also see how rigid he can be and it pretty much negates all the above. Case in point, the way he wriggles his eyebrows as I dip a chicken wing into a pot of bleu cheese dressing. "Careful there, Ang. Once on the lips, forever on the hips."

"Who even says that anymore?" I roll my eyes.

"Will does," says Theo, my dentist brother, reaching for another wing, even though he's already got one on his plate.

Reason number three hundred and four I love Theo – he finds Will as annoying as I do. When we were kids, this united us against him – the middle child and the youngest pitted against the terrifying eldest who was too loud and too brash for his own good – always in trouble at school and not much better at home. Theo and I used to sit at the top of the stairs while Mom and Dad had yet another discussion/argument with Will about "consequences," listening and thanking our lucky stars we weren't on the receiving end of that day's lecture.

"Will, leave your sister alone." Dad's voice is matter of fact. He turns to me. "How are you tonight, Ang? Work treating you okay?"

I nod. "I have a headache, but otherwise it's good. Did I

miss the text that it was Sinclair family wing night? And did anyone remember to order garlic parmesan for me?"

"I put them on the side for you." Dad points to a box on the counter. "I can't take credit, though. I came home and these two were already here, food in hand."

As I move towards the counter, I see Will and Theo exchange a look, then Theo's eyes dart to Dad. It stops me dead in my tracks. All three sets of eyes fix on me and I put my hands on my hips. "Why? What's going on?"

Dad clears his throat, but Theo's the one who speaks. "We wanted to talk to you about this blind date feature you're doing."

Before I can respond, Will adds, "Are you sure it's a good idea?"

"And are you sure it's safe?" Dad asks.

An eighteen-wheeler could fall into the gaping silence between us. They've obviously coordinated their attack here. Because that's what it feels like. An attack. Still, I've learned a thing or two being the youngest – and the only girl – in a roomful of testosterone that is my family and my tone is even when I say, "I'm going out on a few blind dates. It's no different than if I were on Tinder or something."

I give Theo a knowing look because I know for a fact he's on at least two, but he shakes his head. "With online dating, your date doesn't already know where you work. I'm worried that you're unwittingly opening yourself up to a lot of crazies."

"Like, what if someone goes all *Single White Female* on you?" Will adds.

That idea is so ludicrous I ignore it and turn to my dad. "Why is this coming up now? I went on my first date and it was fine. I expect the others to be fine, too."

"Your first date was with Jack Reese." Will sounds a lot like he's rolling his eyes. "If you can't trust him, who can you trust?"

I look at Will, eyes wide. "That's your argument? Do you even know him?"

He shrugs, but it's Theo who answers. "He's one of my patients. He's a decent guy."

I swivel my head towards Theo. "And you can tell this from a ten-minute appointment twice a year?"

"No, but he did some built-in shelving for Dr. Perez earlier in the year, so he was in the office a lot." Theo shrugs like maybe he could have mentioned this before and didn't.

In his defense, why would he? He doesn't know that my mind keeps going back to my date with Jack. And that moment in my office where I dismissed him completely. Before I can do it again, Dad says, "Also, his mother happens to be your boss. If that's not a compelling reason to treat you right, I don't know what is." His voice softens. "What if your other dates aren't as considerate?"

All three of them look at me for an answer. I don't have one, except how inane and misplaced their worry is, so I turn and grab my box of wings from the counter and finish one before asking, "So what do you propose? The wheels are in motion and you have no idea what this takes behind the scenes. Besides the fact this is also my job we're talking about."

"Will and I will take turns shadowing your dates." Theo says this like it's already been decided.

Which, I realize, amongst them, it has. This is why they're all here. I shake my head. "*Pink* has protocol in place and I'll be checking in with Victoria. It's already been decided, so thank you, but I don't need one of my older brothers on my date with me."

"Is Victoria going on your date with you?" Theo asks.

"No, of course not. I'll text her."

"And if you don't?" Theo asks. "What's she going to do?"

Trace my phone via the location-sharing app I agreed to

turn on while I'm on a date. After that, the plan gets a little thin, but I'm not saying that out loud.

"It doesn't matter," Will says. "We'll be at the same place with a date of our own."

"Or without a date," adds Theo.

I shake my head harder this time. "I'm flattered that you care and alarmed that you think I can't actually fend for myself in a public place, but no."

"We know you can fend for yourself," Dad starts.

"I lived in Manhattan for ten years and guess what? I wasn't a nun. I went on dates, I even went on blind dates, and I was fine. I had whole relationships you knew nothing about and I was fine." My voice rises. "I moved in with Eli –"

"And you weren't fine." Theo's voice is soft, but it cuts through my rant like a sword. "We told you he wasn't a great guy, but you didn't listen."

I remember that day like it was yesterday. Will, Theo, and Dad had come to New York for my engagement party and Theo had invited me out for lunch sans Eli under the pretense of having a small family celebration before the big night. We got to Blue Smoke and Dad and Will were waiting. One by one they'd expressed "concern" about my engagement to Eli –he was self-centered; he was distant. Was he really the kind of man I wanted to raise a family with some day? I listened and pretended to consider their points, but I was sure I knew better.

Until it became crystal clear I didn't.

My righteous indignation dies, the flames scalding the back of my throat. Or maybe that's embarrassment. It's hard to tell the difference. I scoop up my box of wings from the kitchen counter and look at the space above Theo's left shoulder as I say, "Fine. I'll let you know tomorrow where I'll be on Friday."

I don't wait for their reply. I take my box of wings and head for my room as quickly as I can without breaking into a run.

Chapter Seventeen

JACK

*N*ever in my life have I been as aware of *Pink* as I have this week. It's everywhere. Or, more accurately, everywhere I go someone's talking about it. Including the two women in front of me in the checkout line at Wegman's.

"I think they should have picked the science teacher," the blond says. "He's a little bit nerdy, but so what?"

Her friend, a redhead, says, "I voted for the chiropractor."

Blondie scrunches her nose. "Eeew, no. Even the programmer was better than him, and he has the market cornered on nerdy."

"I know, but the chiropractor's a widower. I mean, can you imagine being a widower at thirty-five? That's got to be heartbreaking," says Red.

I pull my phone out of the back pocket of my shorts in desperation. Scrolling social media is better than listening to random strangers talk about Angeline's date tonight. I don't give a damn who she's going out with. Tonight or any other night. She made it clear that her write up about our date last week was embellished to build interest in the magazine feature.

I would have sworn she enjoyed it as much as I did, but only a fool chooses to ignore something he's told outright.

"I wish they didn't pick the accountant, though. He's good-looking, but he came across as kind of an ass. I mean, he's an accountant, it's not like he has a reason to be cocky." says Blondie.

"I can't wait to read her write up on Monday," says Red.

"Me neither." Blondie lets out a sigh. "You know he's never going to measure up to Jack, so why can't she just go out with him again?"

I raise my eyebrows and quickly lower my head, pretending to be fascinated by the Greek yogurt in my basket. My photo in *Pink* was from one of Mom's garden parties last year – a far cry from the backwards baseball cap, T-shirt, and cargo shorts I'm wearing now. But better safe than sorry.

Blondie sets her basket on the stand next to the cashier and hands over her shopping bag. That's all it takes for me to decide I don't like her because how hard is it to pack your own damn groceries? But it doesn't mean I tune her out. "We were talking at work about the whole "Blind Date Diaries" thing. I wonder if she has a save set up if things get weird?"

"What do you mean?" I'm glad Red asks because I'm wondering the same thing.

"Like that Bad Date Rescue app or something like that?" Blondie taps her credit card against the card reader and smiles at the cashier as she takes her bag.

It's Red's turn now and she steps up, makes small talk with the cashier, and steps down to pack her items herself. It means she's facing away from me when she speaks and I have to strain to hear when she says, "Well, if she doesn't, she should."

"I know, right? Remember that time I went out with Greg the Gamer?" Blondie rolls her eyes.

And that's where I tune her out. I don't give a shit about Blondie's dates. And I shouldn't be giving a shit about Angeline's. Except I try to remember if I saw Angeline with her phone when we were out and I don't think I did. Aside from taking a few photos of the chocolate, she didn't pull her phone out once.

It's not my problem. I shouldn't care. A big part of me doesn't care.

Until Red says, "The key is to always take your own car. Then you're golden."

She picks up her carrier bag and walks away, leaving me next in line. I glance up at the cashier and force a smile. She's a matronly woman with dyed blond hair, laced with streaks of gray. I'd put her around my mother's age if I had to guess, although I can't picture Victoria Buchanan in polyester any more than I can picture her in a grocery store.

"Good evening. Are you planning a nice weekend?" the cashier asks.

I shrug. I'm working a little and maybe heading out to the lake tomorrow night with Chris and a couple friends. "Nothing special, but it's the weekend, right? How about yourself?"

The cashier grins and it gives me a little kick. I could probably count on one hand the number of people who ask her about her plans and it makes me feel decent to be one of them. "My daughter is having a birthday party for me tomorrow. It's supposed to be a surprise, but she's terrible at keeping surprises." I laugh and she scans my spinach. "I hope you're going to cook something nice with this?"

"Nah, just salad, probably. It's too hot to cook." And my cheap-ass apartment only has a window AC unit in the bedroom, so I'm not doing anything that will make the rest of it hotter.

The cashier nods and lowers her voice. "One of the only reasons I agreed to this surprise party in the first place is because my daughter's house has central air conditioning. It's a blessing in this heat. Sometimes when I get home I sit in the car for a few extra minutes and turn the AC on as high as it will go until I'm actually cold."

I used to do the same thing before I spilled turpentine all over my truck. Now I'm in danger of asphyxiating myself if I drive for too long with the windows up. Speaking of cars... Angeline's smart enough to take her own car, right? I know I drove when we went out, but she should've insisted on meeting me there. The fact that she didn't worries me.

Goddammit, I do not want to be worried about Angeline Sinclair tonight because it doesn't exactly help with trying to forget her. I know she can take care of herself, but being out in public is one thing. Getting into a car with a stranger – especially a stranger who might be perving on your picture in a magazine – is another.

I pay and take my groceries, fishing my phone out of my pocket on my way out the door. I don't text until I'm sitting behind the wheel of my truck because I'm not really sure who to text. I could message Angeline directly, but the chances she won't answer me are high. Erin might tell me, but she'd want to know why I'm asking, and if I tell her the truth, she'd probably change her mind pretty damn quick for fear I'll highjack Angeline's date. I stare at my contacts for a solid minute before my thumbs move over the screen.

Hey, Mom. Do you know where Angeline Sinclair's going on her date tonight?

I bite my lip and press send.

It takes my mother two minutes to respond. *She and Lowell are going to Bella Italia. Not the most inspired choice, but...*

No shit. Who takes a date to an Italian chain restaurant, never mind a date that's going to be written up in a woman's magazine? Say goodbye to ever getting laid again, dude.

My phone buzzes in my hand. *Why are you asking?*

That's a damn good question.

Me: *Curious. I overheard some girls in Wegman's talking about TBDD. That's a good thing, right?*

Mom: *Oooh. Very good. Phil and I are heading out on his boat for a sunset picnic if you want to join?*

Me: *Sorry, I have plans. Another time?*

Mom: *Okay. Have fun!*

I don't bother to respond, but I do glance at the time on my phone. 6:27. I've got time to go home, put my groceries in the fridge, and shower before heading over to Bella Italia. Sergio's beats it any day of the week, but it's not my choice. And I'm feeling like Italian tonight.

Chapter Eighteen

ANGELINE

*D*espite some fervent wishing on my part, my car didn't break down on the way to meet blind date number two. I let out a sigh as I glance in the rearview mirror one more time for mascara smudges before climbing out of my too-reliable Honda Accord and setting off across the parking lot towards the red front door of Bella Italia. My pulse picks up as I pull open the door. Why am I doing this again? Going out with Jack was one thing...

"Good evening. Welcome to Bella Italia. How can I help you?" A young girl in a red blouse and black skirt greets me, her smile wide.

If I'm going to back out, now's the time. I can tell Victoria I got cold feet. She'll understand. But the image of her face when I tell her I bailed before I even saw my blind date flashes through my head. She won't understand that. I open my mouth to speak, then close it as the door opens behind me. The hostess glances up and then back to me. "I'm meeting someone. I'm not sure if he's here yet?"

"You wouldn't be Angeline Sinclair, would you?" A deep voice behind me asks.

Oh boy. I take a deep breath and paste on a smile, speaking as I turn around. "Yes, actually. And are you —" His name dies on my lips.

This is Lowell? Oh. My. No wonder *Pink* readers chose him. His photo doesn't do him justice. Tall with short brown hair, he's wearing the white button down and blue pants I envisioned when I read that he was an accountant. But I definitely didn't predict those broad shoulders. Or that trim waist. And that just-so stubble... Lowell is downright hot.

It takes me a second to realize he's holding his hand out for me to shake. "I'm Lowell McGregor. It's great to meet you."

I take his hand and give a brief shake before letting go. My palms are a little clammy suddenly. "Hi. It's great to meet you, too."

Lowell looks back to the hostess and says, "McGregor, table for two? I booked yesterday."

The hostess looks at her clipboard and gives Lowell a bright smile. She chatters as she leads us to the table, but I'm not listening because my head is spinning a little. Lowell is, like, movie-star handsome. Since when do guys like him live in Rochester, New York? And why is he here as my blind date?

Either the stars are aligning or there's something wrong with him. Oh God. What's wrong with him?

Melissa would tell me not to look a gift horse in the mouth and Jack would... Well, I don't know what Jack would say, but thinking of him makes me feel guilty. Which is ridiculous. I haven't heard from him since he showed up in my office Tuesday afternoon, so it's not like I owe him anything.

Except maybe an apology?

I sit down and realize Lowell is looking across the table at me. Crap. I need to get my head in the game. I take a deep breath and paste on another smile. "So, thanks for doing this."

Lowell nods. "Yeah, of course. Of course. My sister nomi-

THE BLIND DATE DIARIES

nated me, and I didn't even know she'd done it until I got the call telling me I'd been voted in as this week's date."

Oh boy. Does that mean he wants to be here or not? "Wow. Some sister you've got, huh?"

"She's one of a kind." Lowell looks like he might smile but doesn't. "So, tell me how this works?"

"Uh, well, we have a date and then I write about it." A weird little laugh escapes. "That's kind of it, really."

"Okay." Lowell draws the word out into three syllables. "Why?"

"We're trying something different at *Pink*. You know, connecting with our readership, expanding our scope." I shrug like I didn't spend an hour this afternoon rehearsing this exact response with Melissa. "It's a month-long feature, but last week's segment was really popular, so we're off to a great start."

"I read your piece this afternoon." Lowell gives me a look I can't interpret and I swallow down the urge to ask him what he thought. "So, you're doing this as an alternative to all the apps out there?"

"Uh, no." Didn't I just tell him why I'm doing this? Maybe not me, specifically, but it was implied, wasn't it? "I'm doing this for *Pink* mostly."

Lowell nods. "Got it. So tell me about yourself. Are you divorced?"

"Nope." Despite the fact I told Jack the barebones version of my past relationship fail, Eli and Rachel are not blind-date fodder. "I've been busy, focusing on other things. Dating has taken a back seat."

"I understand that. Career can be all-consuming these days, can't it? Or maybe it's that technology can be all-consuming. It's hard to tell." Lowell takes a smart phone out of his back pocket and puts it face down on the table. I feel like he does it to accentuate his point, but I hate phones on the table. Eli always used to keep his phone on the table, claiming he needed to be available in case of emergency, but weekend golf games somehow constituted emergencies, so...

Did Jack have a phone on our date? I don't remember, which is a point in his favor.

"The blessing and the curse of the modern age." I smile again, but it still feels forced. "Is that why you're available for a random blind date your sister set you up on? Because you're busy focusing on your career?"

"Well, Emily said you seemed smart and insightful. Apparently she thinks I could use a little insight." Lowell smiles and it's a very good smile, but it doesn't distract me from the fact he didn't answer my question. Add to that the fact that Lowell doesn't look like the kind of guy who needs to be set up by his sister and it makes me wonder again what he's really doing here.

Just as I'm thinking about how I can find out more about him without appearing too insistent, the waitress approaches our table. "Hi there. I'm Dawn and I'm going to be taking care of you tonight. Can I get you drinks while you look at the menu? A bottle of wine, maybe?"

"We're both driving, so I think we'll skip the drinks tonight, Dawn. I'll have an iced tea and Angeline here will have...?" He looks at me expectantly.

Oh. Okay, I was going to have a glass of wine, but now I'll look irresponsible if I order one. I say, "I'll have a raspberry iced tea, thanks. And can we have some bread, please?"

"No bread for me, thanks," Lowell says quickly.

No wine and no bread? Whoa. I wait for the waitress to move away before I ask, "No bread? Do you follow a gluten-free diet?"

"Not at all, but I try to keep carbs to thirty percent of my diet. I already know I'm planning to have a side of pasta." Lowell lowers his voice like he's telling me a secret. "The angel hair pasta here is amazing. It's the only pasta they make fresh every day."

"Oh, nice. Thanks for the tip. The only Italian I frequent is a mom-and-pop place on Park Ave, Sergio's. Do you know it?" Jack's face comes to mind and I give myself a little mental shake. I'm not out with Jack, although I can't help thinking that if I was, we'd never be at a place like Bella Italia.

Lowell makes a face. "Unpopular opinion, but I hate Park Avenue. It's all boutique shops and overpriced restaurants, like a Greenwich Village wannabe."

Lowell's not wrong, but that's my neighborhood he's talking about. The neighborhood I lived in way before it was cool. "You hate Park Avenue? How is that possible? It has so much charm, and Summer Fest is amazing."

"Summer Fest is fun if you're twenty. By thirty, it's a nightmare." Lowell leans back in his chair, a sardonic smile on his face. "I have a friend who lives down there and he claims it's the best of both worlds, close to the city but still a true neighborhood. Is that your line, too?"

"I'm not going to answer that on the grounds it might incriminate me." I give a tight-lipped smile. Lowell is dismissive, but he's spot on.

"You sound like a lawyer." Lowell grins to soften his words, but doesn't give me a chance to respond before saying, "Emily says you're an editor at *Pink*?"

"I'm the editor, actually." Emphasis on *the* because I work too hard to downplay it.

"Nice gig. I've heard great things about the new magazine format."

"Thanks." I want to ask what things but manage to stop myself. I also want to ask Lowell if he reads *Pink* himself, but he's not really our target demographic. So instead I ask, "You're an accountant, yes?"

"Yes. I do a lot of corporate accounting, but I have a few private tax clients. Did you know –"

The waitress reappearing with our drinks cuts off whatever

Lowell is going to ask. She slides our glasses across the smooth wooden table, then pulls out her pen and order pad. "So, have you decided what you're having tonight?"

Just as I'm about to say no – I haven't even looked at the menu – Lowell says, "I think we'll start with the antipasto, Dawn, and then for a main course I'll have the pollo fungi with a side of angel hair arrabiata, and Angeline will have the sea bass siciliana with a side of angel hair alfredo." Lowell smiles and hands his menu back to Dawn.

Wait. What? Did my blind date just order my food for me?

What. The. Hell?

Dawn turns to me and I'm so taken aback I almost hand my menu back to her, too. I go so far as to lift it off the plate before I say, "Actually, I don't like seafood, so I'm going to have to change that."

"You don't like seafood?" Lowell's tone is incredulous. "Maybe you've never had the right dish."

"Trust me, it's a long-standing dislike." Almost as ingrained as disliking people ordering for me without my input. I smile up at Dawn. "If you can give me a few minutes, I'll take a look at the menu and decide."

Dawn nods and opens her mouth to speak, but before she can say anything, Lowell jumps in and says, "I'd recommend the chicken parmesan. Or the risotto if you're vegetarian. What do you think, Dawn?"

"Yes. Both are excellent choices." Dawn looks a little taken aback by Lowell's insistence. I can so relate to this.

"I'd really like to have a look at the menu if you don't mind?" I address my question to Dawn, who nods again. "And you know what? I'd love a glass of Chianti when you come back?"

Dawn scurries off and I open the menu, peeking up at Lowell over the top. He's picked his phone up off the table and his thumbs fly over the screen. I clear my throat and say, "I just need a minute."

Lowell gives me a vague *mmm* sound from the back of his throat, but he doesn't look up as I scan the menu. I don't really care what I order – as long as it's not fish. It's not like I have much of an appetite. But one thing's for certain. When Dawn comes back, I'm ordering bread too.

Chapter Nineteen

ANGELINE

S ince the wine and fish disagreement, Lowell's been on his phone almost nonstop, so I have a lot of time to check out the restaurant. Which means I see the exact moment Theo comes in and makes his way to the bar, followed five minutes later by...Jack Reese?

What is Jack doing here? And why does my heart leap when I see him? Maybe it's because he looks great in his khaki shorts and a light blue T-shirt that pulls across his shoulders. Or maybe it's because I'm glad he's here?

Am I glad he's here? Judging by the fluttering in my stomach, it sure feels that way.

Jack goes up and clasps Theo on the shoulder, then signals the bartender for a drink. While he waits for his drink he talks to Theo, then suddenly he looks right at me, tipping an imaginary hat. My face flushes and I try to play it cool with a sharp nod of my head, but my smile can't hide my relief. I don't know why Jack's here, but it doesn't feel like a coincidence. Which means...well, I don't know what it means. But I don't think it's bad.

I look up to find Lowell eyeing me, fork poised halfway to his mouth. "Is everything okay?"

Part of me feels like I should try to spark up a conversation now that Lowell's not buried in his phone. I'm working after all and this isn't a real date. But a bigger part of me can't do it. I put my fork down on the edge of my plate and lean in. "I'm fine, but a friend of mine just walked in, and I'm going to go over to say hello."

Lowell frowns at my plate. "You're not finished with your chicken."

Truthfully, I've only taken about three bites because I was a little overzealous with the bread and olive oil when it came, so it's not surprising. "I'm actually pretty full."

Lowell's mouth pinches. "This is why I limit carbs. They don't do you any good."

I'm pretty sure my size eight jeans in the back of my closet would agree, but I shrug and say, "Bread is one of my essential food groups."

Lowell shakes his head slowly, "And that's why you'll struggle to reach your optimal body composition. It's simple math, really."

I straighten in my chair. Optimal body composition? Did he just say that?

Heat rises in my cheeks, a mixture of astonishment and irritation. "Who says I'm not at my optimal body composition already?"

The corner of Lowell's mouth quirks up. "I didn't mean it as a criticism. There's nothing wrong with having your cake and eating it, too, if you're happy with the inevitable consequences."

Wow. Any questions I had about why someone who looks like Lowell needs his sister to fix him up are answered. I place my palms on the table. "You didn't mean that as a criticism either, I guess?"

"There's no need to get upset. Like I said, it's simple math."

"Maybe, but it still sounds a lot like judgment to me." I push my chair back. "I'm going to say hello to my friend, and I won't be coming back to join you. Thank you for dinner."

Lowell's eyes narrow. "Hey, I didn't mean anything by it. Just a little real talk, you know?"

"We met less than an hour ago, Lowell. What makes you think I want or need real talk from you is a conversation I'm not willing to have." My palms press harder into the linen tablecloth, but my voice remains steady and calm. How, I honestly don't know, but I'll be forever grateful because Lowell doesn't warrant the emotional energy of a scene.

Lowell shrugs as I push myself to my feet. "Suit yourself."

"Great. I will." I clench my jaw hard so I won't say anything else and turn towards the bar. My heels make a loud clacking noise on the hardwood floor, reverberating through my legs as I walk, punctuating my anger. By the time I've reached the bar, I'm grinding my teeth so hard I'm surprised I don't have a mouth full of dust.

Jack and Theo are seated with their backs to me and Theo notices me first. Probably because I take his soda out of his hand without asking and bring it to my lips, taking two long swallows before giving it back.

Theo raises his eyebrows. "Go ahead and help yourself."

"Thank you. I owe you." I eye up his cola and he hands it over again.

"I thought you were on a date?" Theo asks.

"I was." I've avoided looking at Jack, but I let myself glance at him as I bring the glass to my lips again. Yep, he looks great up close, too. My heart leaps like an Olympic high jumper.

"And now you're not?" Theo's words come out slowly.

I know it's because he assumes something's wrong and isn't sure whether to ask, so I spit out, "Lowell's an asshole. Apparently he thought I was going to be thinner."

"What the fuck?" Jack leans forward. "Did he say that to you?"

I shake my head and force a deep breath in an attempt to sound calm. The last thing I need is for Jack to get indignant on my behalf. "Not in so many words, but sometimes it's about what you don't say, right?"

"If I need to go have a little chat with him, you say the word, sweetheart," says Jack.

His default 'sweetheart' makes me want to roll my eyes, but I can't deny I appreciate the offer. When I smile, it's weak but genuine. "Nope. But you can buy Theo another soda since I'm drinking his."

"I'm good, so keep your money." Theo laughs and turns to me. "Hey, does this mean I'm officially off babysitting duty?"

I stick out my lower lip in a pout that's not even forced. "No one asked you to babysit."

Theo has the decency to look contrite. "You know that's not what I meant. I'm supposed to be meeting Sophie out at Murphy's, and I wouldn't mind doing that sooner than later."

Theo has been seeing Sophie for about a month but hasn't brought her around because he claims he doesn't want to scare her off. But that doesn't mean I can't meet her, right? "Can I come to Murphy's with you?" I ask.

"Uh, bringing my little sister along on my dates kind of went out when you finished sixth grade." Theo's got a hell-no look in his eyes, but he's also smiling wide.

"Remember when Mom and Dad made you take me to Abbott's with you and Isabella Garcia? I'm not sure which of the three of us was more mortified?"

"I'm pretty sure it was me." Theo shakes his head. "Which is why I'm not taking you to Murphy's. Sorry, not sorry."

"I'll take you," says Jack. Then he holds up one finger. "As long as you promise not to embarrass your brother."

I haven't looked at Jack during this whole exchange, and

when I do his expression doesn't have a trace of cockiness. "Why?"

"Why what?" Jack asks.

My original question was why he didn't want me to embarrass Theo. But the one that comes out of my mouth is, "Why are you willing to take me?"

"I'm not sure." Jack smiles just enough that his cheek dimples on one side. "But maybe don't look a gift horse, sweetheart?"

My eyes dart between Jack and Theo. I can't think about going with Jack without squirming and I can't tell if it's from embarrassment at the way I treated him the other day or something else. Something I don't want to examine too closely right now with both my brother and Jack staring at me, waiting for an answer.

I focus on Theo instead. I want to meet Sophie, but a bigger part of me wants to just go out, have a glass of wine, and forget about the Lowells of the world. Which I can do if Jack drives. I can also get an Uber, but only if I can convince the driver to take me all the way out to the lake.

Jack's voice interrupts my thoughts. "You should see the look on your face. It's just a drink."

"And a ride. I know what a crazy driver you are." I smile a little, but those earlier butterflies in my stomach have morphed into birds playing whack-a-mole on my rib cage.

"As I recall, you were kind of into my crazy driving." Jack laughs and he doesn't look nervous at all, which makes me think I'm the one making this into a thing and he's not given it a second thought.

"Ang is a speed demon," Theo says. "A fact belied by her current choice of car."

I laugh. "My current car was chosen based on cost and availability. If I had the means, I'd have an BMW i8 in a heartbeat."

"Just to warn you, I don't have the Jeep tonight," Jack says. "I have my work truck, which isn't nearly as presentable."

"We can take my car if you want?" The words are out of my mouth before I think about what I'm offering. Isn't the whole point of Jack taking me so I can have a drink? And now I'm offering to drive him.

"Does your car smell like turpentine?" Jack asks.

"No. It probably smells like bagels, though, because I bought some for the weekend, but I think that's a better alternative." I glance over at Theo, who's watching my exchange with Jack. "Okay, Murphy's, it is. You might want to text Sophie and tell her we're coming."

"You promise you're going to be nice?" Theo asks as he pulls out his phone.

"I'll be the epitome of sisterly support." I make a cross over my heart for emphasis.

Theo rolls his eyes and walks on ahead, his thumbs moving over the screen of his phone. I turn to Jack, ready to blurt out an apology until he lowers his voice and says, "Don't be too sisterly, sweetheart."

I laugh and he extends his elbow for me to latch on to. I take it, squeezing my fingers on his warm skin and the apology dies on my lips. I need to apologize for the other day. I know I do. But right now, with my hip knocking against his and that smile on his face mirrored on my own, I don't want to ruin the moment. Because I'm pretty sure it's the best one I've had since last Friday night.

Chapter Twenty

JACK

I drive fast, but Angeline is fucking Danica Patrick. By the time she pulls into a spot at the edge of Murphy's parking lot, I've been white knuckling the edge of my seat for at least ten minutes. Which has its merits because it keeps me from thinking about what the hell I'm doing here in the first place. I don't think Angeline notices how unnerved I am by her driving, but as we get out of the car she flashes me a smile over the roof and says, "You okay there, big guy? I didn't make you nervous, did I?"

I let out a low chuckle. "When was the last time Theo rode with you?"

Angeline comes around the front of the car and shrugs. "Ten years ago, maybe?"

"That explains everything." I laugh again and gesture for her to go first through the sea of cars ahead of us.

Murphy's is packed. No surprise since it's a sunny summer evening, but I prefer Blake's a few miles down along the shore and different from Murphy's in every conceivable way. So what I'm doing here is anyone's guess. Fucking Lowell. I blame him for the turn this night has taken, but especially for the fact I'm ogling Angeline's ass right now as she cuts between the cars. If he can't appreciate the fact that her curves are sexy as hell, he's missing out. Big time.

At least her NASCAR-like driving required enough of her concentration that she didn't ask what I was doing at Bella Italia. But there's nothing stopping her from asking me now. I brace myself as she turns a few feet from the door, raising her voice to be heard over the speakers blaring from the deck. "I haven't been here in years and now I remember why."

I nod. "Want to bail?"

"I want to meet Sophie, but can we make a deal that this is a one-drink stop?" She sticks her hand out for me to shake and I take it.

I'm not the type of guy to talk about sparks and shit. I mean, sure, attraction is hotter with some women than others. but it's usually my cock driving that train, and flirtation and innuendo ride along. Angeline and I haven't said a single flirtatious word since leaving the restaurant, so that jolt I feel when I take her hand surprises me. And judging by the look on her face, I'm not the only one.

We stand hand-in-hand for a good ten seconds before I let go, sounding like an asshole when I say, "It's your show, sweetheart. I'm just along for the ride."

Angeline's face falls and her voice is tight when she says, "Great. Sure. Let's go find Theo and Sophie."

She turns back towards the door and before I can finish kicking myself I grab her wrist. She whirls back to me, but before she can speak, I say, "I'm sorry. That was me being a dick for no good reason. Old habits are hard to break."

Angeline looks down at my fingers circling her wrist and then back to my face. I let go and she smiles. Barely, but it's enough. "Okay. Thank you." Before she turns toward the door, she says, "I owe you an apology for the other day when you stopped by *Pink*. I didn't know what to say to

Mike, so it was easier to pretend I was playing up the fact that I had a great time last week for the article. I'm sorry, too."

She doesn't wait for me to reply before walking through the door. It takes me a full minute to follow and by the time I get to the door, she's already inside.

Murphy's is your typical beach bar – worn wooden floor, a handful of high tables with stools, and a big sliding glass door leading to the deck overlooking the lake. The bar takes up the length of the back wall, so the area we walk into is pretty empty because the crowds are either lining up for drinks or out on the deck enjoying the summer breeze. I place a hand on the small of Angeline's back and say, "I'll get you a drink. What are you having?"

"If I say Malbec will you ask for that, specifically, and not just a red wine? I'm really particular about my wine. If they don't have Malbec, a Blue Moon would be great."

"Blue Moon, huh? That's my beer." It's a tiny coincidence. Miniscule. Not something I should be reading into at all. Just like I shouldn't be reading into the fact that I'm touching her. Again. So much for playing it cool.

Except then she gives me a wide smile and says, "I know." Then, God help me, she bats her eyelashes. "Do you want to share?"

"I think after Lowell, you've more than earned your own beer." Plus, the thought of passing a beer back and forth feels intimate and I don't need any encouragement tonight.

"You're right. Beer counts as carbs, right? I should take a picture of those empties and send it to Lowell." She points to a bunch of beer bottles abandoned on a table.

"Don't waste your time." I almost say something about how she's beautiful the way she is, but the words stick in my throat like clumpy oatmeal. "Why don't you hit the deck and I'll get us beers?"

"Okay. I'll see if I can score some seats." Angeline grins and turns away.

I'm not the only one watching her walk away, judging by the voice beside me who says, "Hey, aren't you the guy from the "Blind Date Diaries"? We all read it in the office this week. Man, she was hitting you up for a second date, but it's a no go, huh?"

I turn to the guy who spoke. He's a little too eager for my liking, and I offer a half-hearted shrug. "No idea what you're talking about, man."

"You're Jack, right? From the story in *Pink*? If not, you look a hell of a lot like him." I give a tilt of my head that this dude takes as an affirmation. "What's she like? The girl? My sister said I should enter as a laugh, but I don't know."

Two things become immediately clear. Number one: this guy has no idea that the woman I'm with is Angeline. And number two: I'm glad. My photo in *Pink* was bad, but Ang's is worse. Her hair is darker than it is now and she's turned away from the camera, looking back over her shoulder like a glamour shot gone wrong. My mom said Angeline picked it herself. I didn't give it a second thought until now.

Angeline's photo has been in the magazine more than a few times. If someone wanted to find out what she really looked like, it wouldn't be that hard. Sure, it might require some online digging, not a lot. But this guy – and probably the majority applying for the "Blind Date Diaries" – isn't really bothered. It's more about them than her.

I turn back to the guy with a shrug. "She's all right. She can be a bit of a bitch, if I'm being honest. Might want to dodge that bullet."

The guy laughs. "Good to know, man. Thanks."

I nod and turn back towards the bar. Right into Angeline, her arms crossed tight across her chest.

"Wow. Thanks." Her voice is thin and tight. "I've never been a bullet to be dodged before."

I shake my head as the guy with all the questions eyes us. "Let's not discuss this here."

"Honestly, I don't know why I thought we could do this." Angeline's eyes are hard. "You know how they say fool me once, blah, blah, blah?"

She takes a step and I grab her elbow. It's not the thing to do when she's pissed at me. Especially when she tries to wrench away and my fingers tighten on her arm. But if she takes two more steps, she's right in front of Mr. Curious over there. "Ang, I promise, it's not what you think."

"Funny, that's what he said." Her face falls for a second, but I blink and those walls are back up. "But bitch is pretty self-explanatory to me."

I don't know if it's because I'm worried that Mr. Curious is going to figure out who Angeline is or because I'm frustrated that I look like an asshole. Again. But I close the space between us and say, "Is this self-explanatory, too?"

Then I kiss her.

Chapter Twenty-One
ANGELINE

*J*ack Reese is kissing me. And my lips – traitors that they are – kiss him back for at least thirty seconds before I pull myself away. Not that I want to pull away because Jack's lips on mine are electric. That's almost as much of a shock as him kissing me here in the first place.

"What the –"

He yanks me to his chest, his hands firm on my back. His voice is low in my ear as he says, "There's a guy over there who's interested in applying for the "Blind Date Diaries". He doesn't know who you are and I'm guessing you want to keep it that way. I also highly doubt you want word to get out that you're here with me."

Maybe my head is still foggy from that kiss because I don't understand. "Why?"

"Because as far as everyone else is concerned, you're out with Lowell right now."

Oh, right. My date with Lowell feels like it was a lifetime ago. "Okay. And as far as you're concerned?"

"I don't want *Pink* to fold any more than you do. Imagine my mother unemployed. She'd be all up in my business faster than you can say varnish and trust me when I say I just got her out of my business." Jack chuckles as he rolls his eyes. His tone is playful.

Why my heart free falls is anyone's guess. It settles somewhere around my stomach as I say, "Yep. You're right. No one wants that."

Jack glances over to where our gawker was supposedly standing and says, "I think we're in the clear."

He doesn't let go of me and I make no move to put any space between us. Maybe that's why my mouth goes dry when his eyes meet mine. I try to swallow and let my teeth scrape over my bottom lip. It's pure nerves on my part, which ratchet up when Jack leans down and says, "Are you trying to drive me crazy, sweetheart?"

Judging by the obvious sign of his arousal pressing into my stomach, I don't think he's talking about me driving him crazy in my usual way. I widen my eyes and try – without much success – to keep my lips from tilting up. "I don't know what you're talking about."

Jack's hands tighten on the small of my back, pulling me closer. "Don't you?"

God, what am I doing? This is Jack Reese, for crying out loud. And unlike two weeks ago when we were on the verge of a hate fuck in his kitchen, this is pure attraction. Which I totally blame on hormones or pheromones or whatever kind of gnomes are responsible for this kind of thing. I lick my lips again. "Okay. Maybe a little."

"Why?" All traces of joking have disappeared from Jack's face, and I swear there's more heat contained in that one word than I ever thought possible.

I know what he's asking. Just like I know where an honest answer will lead us. I'm not sure I'm ready to be that honest, so I say, "I haven't been in this situation in a long time."

"What situation is that?" Jack asks.

He knows damn well the kind of situations I have been in, so it's not like his question is unexpected. I swallow, even though my tongue feels like a discarded tea bag in my mouth. I have two choices here – the brave one or the wimpy one. I know which one I should go with – my pheromones/hormones/garden gnomes are begging for it – but I wonder if I used up all my bravery eight months ago when I walked out on Eli. That thought is all it takes for me to wimp out and say, "Kissing a guy I like in a bar. It happens less than you think."

"How do you know what I think?"

"I don't." I manage a swallow and add, "Sweetheart."

One corner of Jack's mouth tilts up. Then the other as his mouth splits into a grin. "That's my line."

"Not anymore." I grin at him in reply and I don't even know why. All I know is that he's still got his arms wrapped around me and I like it.

"I'm going to kiss you again. Everywhere." His tone is so easy he sounds like he could be ordering a pizza, until he adds, "Unless you say you don't want me to, in which case I'll never touch you again."

"That's a bit all or nothing, isn't it?" My pulse picks up a notch.

"I like a woman who knows what she wants." Jack's voice drops and his lips brush my ear. "Even better if she's willing to ask for it."

His breath on my skin causes tiny shivers down my back. "I was wrong before. I thought that was the moment to be brave, but it's this one, isn't it?"

"Brave?" Jack doesn't release his hands on my back, but he straightens. I feel the absence of his body pressed against mine. "Is there something you need to tell me, sweetheart? Because brave isn't the word I had in mind here."

Jack's eyes fill with concern and I feel the flirtation slipping away like sand in an hourglass. Shit, shit, shit. I want this and if it goes to hell right now, I have no one to blame but myself. I lower my voice and press my chest into his as I stand on my tiptoes to say, "Like I said before, it's been a long time since I've been in this situation. I can't remember the last time I said the phrase 'next time I'm in your kitchen, I'm not leaving until we're both satisfied.'"

"Jesus Christ." Jack sucks in a breath and I see his Adam's apple bob in his throat. "Have you ever said that phrase?"

"I'll never tell." I smile up at him. "But depending on how that goes, we can move to the next room."

Jack's hand moves to clasp mine. His grip is so tight it's almost painful, but I don't pull away. "Did you still want to see Theo while we're here?"

I nod. "That's what we came here for, isn't it?"

Jack laughs and it's rich and deep. "I thought so, but now I'm not so sure, sweetheart."

"Well, I guess the sooner we find Theo, the sooner we can find out." I squeeze Jack's fingers and pull my hand away as I turn towards the door leading to the deck, calling over my shoulder, "And if you could get me that Blue Moon, it wouldn't hurt."

Jack's laugh follows me out the door and my own grin is plastered on my face. This night has improved tenfold from where it was an hour ago. And I have a feeling it's just getting started.

Chapter Twenty-Two

ANGELINE

The minute I step into the sea of people on Murphy's deck, panic sets in. Not panic at finding Theo because if I don't meet Sophie tonight he won't mind. But panic about whatever comes next with Jack.

What does come next with Jack?

I pretty much just propositioned him. Which was one thing when I did it two weeks ago at the Old Toad. It's another to do it sober, knowing he's into me. Because behind all that swagger, I see it. Whether he wants me to or not.

I reach into my bag and let my fingers run over the smooth surface of my phone. It's times like this I wish I had more girl-friends. Another tick in the Things I Regret About Eli column is that I become that girl – the one who dropped her entire social circle in favor of her high-flying boyfriend. But, thank God I have one girlfriend I can text before I self-combust.

I pull my phone from my bag and type: *Jack Reese kissed me.*

Melissa texts back immediately. *Jack Reese? How? I thought you were on a blind date?*

Me: *Long story. But Jack Reese kissed me!!*

Melissa: *How was it?*

Me: *Good?*

"Oh good, you made it." Theo's voice makes me clasp my hand over the screen of my phone and my eyes fly up. He's doing that whole sarcasm-with-a-smile thing he does, but his smile is wary.

Due, no doubt, to the woman next to him. Whose long black hair and enviable cheekbones haven't changed since high school, although now she wears funky red glasses and is holding my brother's hand. Considering I've moved back to my hometown, I don't see many people from Brighton High School, which is how I like it. So seeing a former classmate latched onto my brother is just plain strange. "Sophie Chen? You're the Sophie who's dating my brother?"

She gives the close-mouthed smile I remember. "Surprise. How are you, Angeline?"

"I'm good. How are you?" I don't wait for her to answer before saying to Theo, "Why didn't you tell me you were dating someone I went to high school with?"

Sophie answers. "It's my fault. I thought it might be weird. We weren't exactly friends back in the day."

Her words are truthful, but on the heels of the realization I had earlier about my lack of girlfriends, they hit me like a punch in my stomach. I wince. "I know. I was..."

The truth is, I don't even know how to finish that sentence. I was popular and you weren't? Yes. I thought I was all that and a bag of chips? Two for two, anyone want to go for three?

"You were part of the popular crowd and I wasn't. I blame the dried fish I used to eat in the cafeteria." Sophie laughs. "Omega three's or not, what was I thinking? That was social suicide."

I'd forgotten Sophie even did that. "I can't eat fish at all, so more power to you." I make a face then ask, "So how did you two meet?"

"Sophie's a flight attendant and we met when I was traveling to a pain management conference in Michigan," says Theo.

"That's cool. Wow." I'm trying to picture Sophie handing out drinks at thirty-thousand feet and I can't quite do it.

"Not the most exciting story, but we're here now, right?" Sophie squeezes Theo's hand and beams up at him.

His smile is wider than I've ever seen. If not ever, than at least in the past eight months. Not that I go around actively thinking about Theo's smile, because I don't. But that wattage is hard to miss.

"I think it's great. Really" I furrow my brow at Theo. "But I can't believe you didn't tell me."

Theo raises his eyebrows. "Like you didn't tell me that Jack Reese would be riding shot gun on your date tonight?"

"I didn't know. I haven't talked to him since Tuesday." I've been so caught up in kissing Jack and flirting with him that I haven't given his appearance at Bella Italia a second thought. "Maybe Victoria sent him when she realized how shoddy our app check in really was?"

"It didn't seem that way to me. Why don't you ask him?" Theo nods over my shoulder and I don't have to turn around to know that Jack is approaching.

"Jack Reese," Sophie says softly with a little nod. "We went to college together."

"You did?" What are the odds?

"We went to SUNY Albany." Sophie flashes her teeth in what could either be a grimace or a smile. "He dated my room-mate for a bit."

I don't get to think about it anymore before I feel an arm snake over my shoulder.

"Here you go. The wine didn't seem like it would be up to your standards, so Blue Moon it is." Jack holds the beer out for me to take. As I turn his eyes widen and he says, "Holy shit. Sophie Chen. How are you?"

Sophie's smile is way wider for Jack than it was for me. (Not that I'm noticing. Not really.) "I'm good. How are you doing? It's great to see you live and in person."

Jack blushes and it's as cute as it is unexpected.

"I'm really good. I ran into Stephanie a few weeks ago. She was home visiting her mom. Do you keep in touch with her?" Jack asks.

"Not really. I lost track of her when she moved to Hong Kong," Sophie says.

"Apparently she's in Germany now and is some big shot in the finance world. She tried to explain what she does, but she kind of lost me at FTSE." Jack turns his attention to me. "Stephanie was Sophie's old college roommate. We dated for a while before Stephanie realized she could do better."

"Well, I'm not sure Asher Shaw was an improvement," Sophie says with a laugh.

"Sophie just mentioned that. It must be six-degrees-of-separation-day, because Sophie and I actually went to high school together." I half-expect Sophie to make some remark about me or my friends. Some of them were quintessential mean girls and judging by what she said earlier, I doubt Sophie and her dried fish were immune from their taunting.

"Ang was one of the beautiful people in high school," says Sophie.

I blush red to the roots of my hair as Theo adds, "And she racked up hours in front of the mirror to earn it. I remember Will and I pounding on the bathroom door because she'd locked herself in there to curl her hair. Like there wasn't another mirror in the house."

"Hey, it was hard work trying to look like Cindy Crawford before eight a.m." I take a long swallow of my beer and rack my brain for a change of subject. But the six-degrees-of-separation thing has thrown me.

"Hell, it's hard to look like much of anything before eight

a.m.," Jack says with a chuckle. He nudges me with his hip. "Is your Blue Moon satisfactory, sweetheart?"

Jack just threw me a save and I'm pretty sure he knows it, so I bat my eyes at him. "It's very good, thank you, darling. You know if you keep calling me that, people are going to talk."

"I say we give them something to talk about then." Jack puts his arm around my shoulder and lets loose another laugh. It's easy and unselfconscious. Theo says something and everyone laughs, but even though I join in, I don't hear what he said. I'm too focused on the feel of Jack's fingers on my skin, my body tucked into his, and how great it feels.

Chapter Twenty-Three

JACK

The first thing Angeline says to me as we leave Murphy's is, "I was kind of a bitch in high school."

"You don't say." I didn't know teenage Angeline, but I know Sophie. If she didn't like Angeline, it's probably legit. Not that Sophie would say that outright – she's way too nice – but her nonverbal cues were hard to miss.

"Is that why you hated me when we met?" Angeline's tone is matter of fact.

"Whoa. First of all, I didn't know you in high school, and second, who said I hated you?" It's been the exact opposite, but obviously I've done a stellar job of keeping that to myself.

Angeline shrugs. "No one, but you can tell. I can tell."

"Do you still think I hate you?" I stop next to a white Camry parked under a light so I can see her face more clearly when she answers. Because if she answers yes after tonight, that's bad. On the surface tonight has been just a drink with Theo and Sophie and a few laughs, but it feels like things between us have shifted.

Or maybe that's a sign of how loose my grasp is on what's really going on here, judging by the way Angeline furrows her brow at me. It feels like a week passes before she says softly, "No. I don't think so."

"I don't hate you. I've never hated you." I look up at the sky like the right words might be written there. They're not. "I like you. A lot."

"I'm glad." Angeline smiles and I can't help noticing the shy sexy way she bites her lip. Correction: my dick can't help noticing. "Why were you at Bella Italia earlier?"

I think about lying, but I can't. "I didn't like the idea of you being out with some random guy with no back up."

"I was fine." Angeline's eyes are steady on mine.

"I know." I do know, but still. "But what if you weren't?"

"I was fine. *Pink* has safety protocols in place, and I would never be in danger." Angeline's tone is firmer this time. "Please tell me you know that."

"I do. I just −" I blow out a long breath because, truthfully, I didn't know about the safety protocols. Then again, I didn't ask, did I? "I wanted to make sure."

For a second I think Angeline is going to push me to tell her why. But then her face breaks into a wide smile and she says, "Well, thank you. I appreciate it."

"Anytime, sweetheart." The tightness in my chest loosens as I laugh. "So, what do you want to do now?"

Angeline glances at her watch and says, "It's early. You could still get your second date of the night in."

"Really?" My smile fades.

She shrugs. "Sure. Why not?"

It takes me two seconds to decide. But it's not really a decision at all. "Okay then. Let's go."

Angeline's face falls. "Sure. Okay. I only had one beer in there, so I can drive and drop you off so you can pick up your car."

"Thanks, but I don't need my car." I raise my eyebrows like I'm looking at her over the rim of imaginary glasses. "And I'm not letting you drive. I don't care if you were drinking water all night, I can't stomach you driving on 495 like it's your personal NASCAR track."

"Bossy." Angeline scowls. "So you're taking me home?"

"No." Am I'm really doing this? I'm not sure what *this* is, but I know there's no going back from it, and the words that come out of my mouth seal the deal. "I thought we could head over to McCann's and you could have a drink while I grab a burger because I'm starving. If you want a burger, too, that's not a problem."

"You want to go to McCann's?" Angeline's tone is unreadable.

I've got no choice but to go all in. Hell, I kissed her with less thought than this. But maybe because that was spontaneous and this isn't, my stomach churns. I continue like she hasn't spoken. "Or, if you don't want to go to McCann's, there's always Nick's downtown and Mount Hope Cemetery. That was my original plan for last week's date, but I wasn't sure you'd go for it."

"As much as I love a garbage plate, I'm not sure I can stomach one now. Besides, isn't the cemetery closed this time of night?"

"Sure, but there are always ways around that." I shrug. "Or there's plan C."

"Plan C?" Angeline raises her eyebrows at me.

"My mom and Phil took his boat out earlier, but I'm sure they're back now. We can always head to the marina and kick back there."

Angeline nods slowly. "I like plan C the best so far, but I'm worried about running into Victoria. What if she and Phil decided to do the same thing?"

They almost never stay at the marina after they dock, but Angeline's right. There are no guarantees they won't be there, and no way to know without texting my mom or showing up to take our chances. "Good point. Plan D then."

"Didn't you offer to show me your woodshop?" Angeline asks.

"I did." And I expected her to take me up on it when hell froze over, but here we are. "It's not glamorous, but it's air conditioned. And my mother will definitely not be there."

Angeline laughs. "Sold. But there's probably no burger from McCann's there."

"We can stop at Wegman's for beer and I'll grab something. I was actually there earlier tonight, but I'm pretty sure I don't want anything I bought." I take a deep breath in. "Is that our plan D then? My place with beer?"

"That's our plan unless you object. I'm kind of inviting myself over, aren't I?" Angeline's expression falters.

Sure. But I want her there. More than I've wanted anything in a long time. "Hey, Ang, you want to come over to my place? We can get some beer and I can show you my restorations?"

I wriggle my eyebrows at her and she laughs. It feels like a victory.

"I bet you say that to all the girls," she says. I know she's kidding, but it feels like the kind of joke that might not actually be a joke, and her words fall into a chasm between us. So much for putting her at ease. She stutters, "I mean, maybe. I don't know, and even if you did, it's none of my business, right?"

I put my hand on her shoulder. "Stop. Come over. Please. I want you to. I want *you* to."

Her green eyes look up at me and her shoulders drop as she nods and says, "Okay."

I reach down and take her hand, holding my other out, palm up. "But you need to hand over the keys because there's no way in hell I'm going to survive another ride down 495 with you."

"I'm insulted by that, you know." She side-eyes me but digs the keys out of her purse. Before she hands them over, she says,

THE BLIND DATE DIARIES

"I don't turn these over lightly, especially to men who insult my driving. So this is me officially noting you owe me."

"What do I owe you?" I raise my eyebrows.

"I don't know. I'll decide." She drops the keys into my outstretched hand and I close my fingers around them so she can't change her mind.

"You let me know, sweetheart, and we'll see what we can do." I grin as I say it and she laughs. But the truth is, I can't think of anything she'd ask for that I wouldn't agree to.

And I do mean anything.

Chapter Twenty-Four

ANGELINE

*F*act: Going grocery shopping with someone is unexpectedly intimate. The whole time we're walking around Wegman's I keep noting where Jack's glance lingers. He buys two six-packs of Blue Moon, but his fingers flicker over the bags of chips, the end cap display for shampoo and conditioner, and boxes of Cheez-its. He ends up buying a turkey sub from the deli counter and a bag of barbecue chips along with the beer, but I wonder what he would have bought if I wasn't there. I don't ask because that feels even more intimate, but the whole thing puts me in a weird frame of mind. By the time Jack unlocks the door to his woodshop – which looks a lot like a repurposed garage – I'm worried this was a bad idea.

Before I can voice my hesitation, he flicks a switch on the wall and light floods the room. It's not a big space, but it's crammed full of furniture in various stages of completion, stacks of wood, a couple red toolboxes, and even a white photographer's screen. For how full it is, there's an order to it I can see even from my place by the front door, and I spy a worn armchair and small metal table in the back corner with a coffee cup on it.

"Wow. This is incredible." My eyes find the Jacobean sideboard Jack told me about and I walk over and stroke the smooth wood. "This is the piece you're restoring, right? It's amazing."

"Thanks." Jack steps up beside me, his bare arm brushing mine. "It was a mess when I got it. Someone had painted it white."

"How awful. Why?" I think I must look appropriately appalled because Jack laughs.

"Who knows? Why do people ever paint real wood?"

"Uh oh. When I lived in Manhattan, I had a white painted dresser." I wince. "To be fair it, was expensive. The whole shabby chic trend, you know."

"Yeah." Jack rolls his eyes. "Where suckers pay extra for something mass produced that's trying to look like it was rescued from your grandmother's basement."

Guilty as charged. I'm pretty sure if I told Jack how much that dresser cost he'd keel over on the spot. I shrug and glance around the room. "Anything here you rescued from your grandmother's basement?"

"Nah. My grandmother gave me all of her stuff years ago when she moved into a senior living center. She had a thing for mahogany, which is nice but not my thing. I kept a few pieces but sold most of it." I look around again and Jack adds, "It's upstairs. This is just my workspace. I try to move finished pieces out of here pretty quickly."

"So you live upstairs? Here?" I furrow my brow because I've been to Jack's apartment and I don't remember seeing a workshop.

"Yep. When you were here last time, we came in the front." He chuckles. "You should see the look on your face."

"What?" My cheeks flush and Jack 's hand skims my hip as I turn towards him, which makes me flush a little bit more.

"You've got second thoughts written all over your face. But

don't worry, sweetheart, I won't hold you to staying." Jack's mouth is still smiling, but it doesn't reach his eyes.

I feel frustration tickle my chest, but my voice is soft when I ask, "Why do you do that?"

"Do what?"

"Put words in my mouth that imply you're not good enough?"

Jack waits five breaths to answer me. I know because I count the number of times his chest rises and falls. Then he says, "If I said I don't know, would you believe me?"

"No."

"Maybe that's why I like you." Jack lets loose a low laugh. "You can't bullshit a bullshitter."

I see what he's doing so clearly it's almost painful. Like getting glasses after months of not realizing you need them. I'm tempted to push him to say it, but I'm not sure either of us are ready for that. Instead I say, "Who are you calling a bullshitter, exactly?"

"Looking at you, Ms. I-Was-A-Little-Bit-Of-A-Bitch-In-High-School." Before I can protest, Jack continues, "For the record, high school's a nightmare. It's amazing any of us come out intact."

"True that. Speaking of, what's the scoop on Sophie Chen? Is she going to be good for Theo?"

Jack nods. "She's good people. Or at least she was back in the day and she still seems pretty genuine."

"They seem happy. Theo hasn't dated anyone in a long time."

"What about you? When was the last time you dated anyone?"

"Uh, I was out on a date earlier tonight, you may recall?" I know that's not what Jack is asking, but I don't want to talk about Eli. I try not to even think about him. Before he can press me, I ask, "What about you?"

"Aside from our not-so-blind date, I'm woefully out of practice." Jack grins.

I burst out laughing. "Woefully? That sounds serious."

"You have no idea, sweetheart." Jack's hand finds my hip
again and stays there this time.

His touch is so light it's barely there. But damn if my voice
isn't breathy when I say, "You should do something about that."

"I intend to." He nods and his grip tightens a bit on my hip.

Is it possible for all of the nerve endings in your body to
converge on one place? For the record, I think it is.

"You should. I mean, I'm sure you could find a date pretty
easily, right? I mean, maybe not tonight, but −"

"Why do you do that?" Jack cuts me off with an emphasis
on the *you*.

"Because I don't know how to shut up when I get nervous."
I force a swallow even though my throat is dry. "And I'm
nervous."

"Are you worried I might kiss you again?" Jack's voice drops
a notch.

"I'm more worried how much I want you to kiss me again."
I swear, my heart is racing faster than my Honda down 495.

"So which is it? More worried or more wanting?" Jack tips
his head just a little and I feel his breath on my cheek.

The latter.

I don't know if I say it out loud because in the next minute
his lips claim mine. I know he kissed me earlier, but this? This
is a first kiss. The kind you remember the next day, the next
year. The next lifetime. His lips are soft on mine, unhurried as
his hand wraps around my back. The other cups my cheek and
his thumb traces my jawbone. It's not until I wind my arms
around his neck that he deepens the kiss, letting his tongue
caress my bottom lip. It's languid and sensual, like we have all
the time in the world and he's savoring this. Us.

My mouth opens to let him in, and I press my chest to his

and tangle my fingers in his hair. I let out a small moan in the back of my throat and Jack pulls gently away.

"I should probably warn you. My neighbors are nosy as hell." He tilts his head to the side and my eyes follow. I didn't even realize there was a window and I start to pull away, but Jack's hand remains firm on my back. "We can either stay here or you can come upstairs."

"Upstairs to your apartment upstairs?"

Jack nods. "I promise not to bite, sweetheart."

My mouth twists with the attempt to not laugh. "Well, that's a shame."

Jack's gaze heats up so much I wonder how I ever used the term ice blue to describe his eyes. But he doesn't say anything, just pulls my hand towards the back of the shop and up the stairs.

Chapter Twenty-Five

ANGELINE

*W*hen we get to the top of the stairs Jack pushes the door open and backs me against the wall, his mouth hard on mine. I'm having total déjà vu, except for the part of me that wants to relish this. That's new. I kiss my way towards Jack's ear as I say, "I thought you were hungry."

Jack pulls away and looks at me. "I am, sweetheart. Can't you tell?"

"No, like properly hungry." I pause. "For food."

"I was, but I forgot all about that." Jack pulls further away. "I feel like you're having second thoughts?"

I'm not. That said, I don't know why I'm slowing things down. I half-suspect it's the fact that we're in the kitchen. Again. "Definitely not. But do you think we could go inside? We don't have the best track record here."

Jack winces. "Right. Of course. I don't have AC, but the windows have been open all day and it's not too hot in here."

He tugs at my hand and I follow him across the hardwood floor, taking in the details of his apartment. The kitchen is cozy and clean, with not even a glass in the sink, and we pass a tall wooden tea chest in the hallway en route to the living room.

The tan sofa looks well worn, but Jack even has matching throw pillows I can't help noticing.

"Wow, look at you, Mr. House Beautiful." I grin up at him. "I like what you've done with the place."

"My mother calls it garage sale chic." Jack gestures to the sofa. "Have a seat and make yourself at home. Can I get you anything?"

I sit but don't let go of Jack's hand. My earlier hesitation has gone — maybe it really was bad vibes from our previous encounter in the kitchen — and I pull him down beside me. "I think I have everything I need."

Jack's palm rests on my thigh and his expression is serious as he says, "If you aren't comfortable here, say the word. Just because we started something, doesn't mean we have to finish it."

"So if I wanted to watch TV, you'd be cool with it?" A smile plays around my mouth.

But Jack's expression stays funeral serious. "Absolutely. Unless you want to watch a DC Comics film, because I'm a Marvel man all the way."

"Are you now?" My grin is wide. "Any chance of me seeing your hammer?"

Jack laughs. "Literally or figuratively?"

I shrug and move so I'm straddling Jack's thighs. Like the first time I was here, I'm wearing a skirt and it rides up on my thighs. But unlike before, I feel like I'm the one in control. It's a heady feeling and I lean in, brushing my breasts against Jack's chest as my lips graze his.

His hand circles around to the back of my neck and he pulls me closer. Before his mouth meets mine, he looks into my eyes. It feels like he's asking permission and I offer a subtle nod.

Then we're kissing. It's the opposite of our kiss downstairs, but twice as intense. It feels like seconds before my blouse is off and Jack's fingers are working their way over the lace of my bra. He gently pinches my nipple and I moan.

"You like that, sweetheart?" Jack's voice is a low growl.

I respond by bucking up against his erection, which is pressed firmly against the neediest part of me. It's Jack's turn to moan and he thrusts his hips in reply and I gasp.

"Tell me you have a condom." My voice is breathy and high as my fingers move to the button of Jack's shorts.

Jack's hand closes around my wrist. "Are you sure you're sure?"

I swallow hard and nod, and from that minute on our mouths and hands are everywhere. At some point, I pull Jack up from the sofa and his shorts join my blouse and skirt on the floor. My fingers slip inside the elastic of his boxer briefs and he pulls away from where he's kissing me behind my ear and says, "God, I want you, Angeline."

"I want you, too." As I speak, Jack's finger plunges inside of me and I gasp out, "Now. Please."

I yank down Jack's boxer briefs and he straightens. He's still wearing his T-shirt and I tug impatiently at the hem, which makes him chuckle. My hands eagerly scrape along his abs as he says, "Are we moving this to the bedroom?"

I shake my head. "No."

I can't say why I don't want to go to the bedroom, but thank God Jack doesn't push it. Instead, he sits down on the couch, raising an eyebrow at me as he grabs a condom off the side table. "Do you want to put this on me?"

"Nope." I bite my lip. "I want to watch."

"Jesus." Jack's breath catches in his chest. But he's not the only one. I watch him stroke himself in anticipation of slipping the condom on and my hand goes between my legs to my slick center. Jack sees me do it and I swear his gaze might scorch my skin, it's so hot. Once he makes sure the condom is in place he says, "Keep doing that and come over here."

He doesn't need to ask twice. I take a step and straddle his thighs, sliding up his erection until his cock teases my entrance. I expect him to plunge into me, but instead he winds one hand behind my neck and fingers me with his other as he murmurs, "Are you going to let me make you come, sweetheart?"

"Yes." My response is almost a whimper.

Jack eases himself inside me, and I have to suck in a breath at first because adjusting to the feeling of him inside of me is a kind of marvelous torture. Until it becomes simply marvelous.

Our bodies move like they were made for each other. We match each other thrust for thrust and when I'm close, Jack eases me off him and bends me over the arm of the couch. This time, there's no hesitation as he enters me, and I'm not positive, but I might see stars when I come.

What I am positive about? When Jack and I are snuggling under a sheet on the couch afterwards, his lips grazing my forehead, it's the most content I've felt in a long, long time.

Chapter Twenty-Six

JACK

he problem with working for yourself is that when you've scheduled jobs out of town, you have to go, personal life be damned. Case in point, the past two days I've been up in the Adirondacks building custom bookshelves for a client with a summer home up there. It's the kind of work I love and the fact that I got to stay in their guest house on the lake free of charge? Ideal, right?

So why I've driven like a bat out of hell to get back to Rochester by mid-afternoon can only be attributed to one thing. Make that one person. I pull into the parking lot behind Oh My Bagel and pull my phone from my pocket to glance at my texts with Angeline from last night.

Me: *Are you up for coming camping with me up here sometime?*

Angeline: *Camping??? I'm sorry, I think you meant to send this to someone else?*

Me: *I meant it for you, sweetheart. I promise I'll serenade you around the campfire. I play a badass Twinkle, Twinkle Little Star on the guitar.*

Angeline: *Hmmm. Will there be s'mores?*

Me: *And an air mattress.*

Angeline: *Just one?*

Me: *Just one.*

Angeline: *Suddenly I'm intrigued.*

I grin at the screen, imagining her face as she types, though I stop short of admitting that little twisty thing her mouth does and the way her eyes narrow are cute. I mean, hell, I know I've got it bad when I'm so impatient to see her I'm willing to risk running into my mother at *Pink*.

I glance around in case Victoria's nearby as I hop out of my truck and cross the parking lot towards Oh My Bagel. It's past lunchtime so there's not much of a line and Chris is the only one at the counter. There are a couple other people working – a guy is sweeping up and a girl is making coffee – but with his eyes trained on the door, Chris sees me immediately.

"Hey. What are you doing here? Can't resist a sandwich of the day? I have a great one for you to try. My Hammy Vice – ham, lettuce, tomato, pepper jack cheese, and spicy mustard," Chris says.

I shake my head. "Can I have my roast beef special and something for Angeline? What will she go for?"

Chris puts a plastic-gloved hand to his chin. "Hmmm. How about a Celine Dijon? Chicken, spinach, and melted Swiss with honey Dijon mustard on a whole wheat bagel?"

"Sold." I watch as Chris slices the bagels and starts assembling the sandwiches. "Do you stay up at night thinking of these names, man?"

"No. Believe it or not, they come to me on the spot. One of the joys of creative living." Chris doesn't even crack a smile when he says this.

I know better than to laugh, but I can't help grinning. "Yeah. Must be."

"So, Angeline, huh? Did the Brie My Baby win her over?" Chris asks as he puts Angeline's sandwich in the oven.

"I don't think so, but maybe." I fish my wallet from my pocket. "I'm not sure I'd say she's won over yet."

I mean, yeah, sex is a step forward for sure, but I'm not naïve enough to think we're a couple now. No matter how much I'd like us to be.

"Well, one of you is, judging by the fact that you're in here getting her lunch on a Wednesday afternoon." Chris wraps my sandwich in paper and hands it to me. "And surprising her with it, too."

It seems like a great idea until I'm standing in the foyer at *Pink*, two sandwiches in hand, asking the receptionist to call Angeline and let her know I'm here. When the call goes directly to voicemail, it starts to feel like not such a good idea. Then Angeline walks into the foyer wearing a navy blue suit, a stack of folders in hand, and says, "Sarah, I need you to take a look through these sales figures and rank our advertisers by..." She pauses, her eyes widening. "Jack? Hi. What are you doing here?"

That's when me stopping by morphs into feeling like a bad idea, because she doesn't look pleased to see me and she sounds even less so.

"I stopped by Oh My Bagel to grab some lunch on my way home and I thought maybe you could use a Celine Dijon." I hold out the sandwich. "You seem busy, so I'll let you get back to work."

"Things are a little crazy today with the board meeting tomorrow, but come on in." To Sarah she says, "I need an Excel spreadsheet with advertisers ranked by total spend, and if you could add two columns to include the average ad size and frequency, that would be great. We're looking for trends and opportunities to upsell."

Sarah nods and Angeline hands the folders over, then turns on her heel back towards her office. There's a low buzz in the office that's not usually present and when we enter Angeline's office, she doesn't close the door before she heads behind her desk and perches on the edge of her chair. I sit in the chair across from her and the feeling that I shouldn't be here intensifies.

"Is, um, everything okay?" I'm not even sure what I'm asking, but this Angeline isn't the same woman who was texting me last night.

"Yes, it's just that Mike pulled the advertising numbers for the board meeting tomorrow and the "Blind Date Diaries" isn't doing as well as we'd hoped." Angeline unwraps her sandwich but doesn't move to take a bite. "I mean, it's not over yet, so there's still time, but it's not encouraging, you know?"

It's not a real question and I don't bother to answer, but one thing is clear. I need to get out of here pronto so she can get on with it. Just as I put my hands on my knees to rise to my feet, Melissa walks in, saying, "Erin pulled the details on the nominations for this week. There are a couple good ones, and I say we fudge it so we get the guy with the maximum wow factor."

Melissa doesn't even notice me until she's right next to my chair and both surprise and guilt flash across her face. "Oh, hey, Jack. Sorry, I didn't know you were here."

"Maximum wow factor, huh? Who knew?" I've been so caught up in Angeline that I forgot all about the fact that she has two more dates to get through.

Two more dates who aren't me, despite everything that's happened between us.

"Desperate times, desperate measures, right?" Judging by the tightness in her expression, Angeline knows exactly what I'm thinking.

Melissa's eyes dart between the two of us. "When you're done, Ang, come over to Erin's desk because she's got everything already up on her screen to mock-up tomorrow's issue."

"Give me a few minutes," Ang says, but any hope I had of

getting those few minutes is blown by her phone buzzing on her desk and her frowning at the screen.

Melissa gives a quick nod and scurries out. I'm still facing Angeline, but hear the door click behind me, and say a silent thank you. "Look, sorry I just stopped by. I didn't realize things were so busy for you."

"Yeah." Ang's attention is still on her phone and she pries her gaze away. "Sorry. It's all a little manic."

"Do you want to grab a bite later, maybe?" Before I even finish speaking, Angeline is shaking her head.

"I can't. The board meeting tomorrow has everyone stressed and I have to work tonight." Maybe it's childish, but I look for a trace of disappointment in Angeline's face. There isn't one.

"Yeah, of course. No problem, sweetheart." I stand, but before I'm even fully vertical, Angeline's head snaps up.

"Don't do that." Her tone comes out sharp.

It takes a lot of self-restraint not to snap back at her, and my tone is even as I say, "Not trying to do anything except getting out of your hair."

Angeline tugs at her ponytail and sighs. "Jack, I'm sorry, I just need to –"

I step towards the door. "I know. I'm out of here. Good luck with your board meeting tomorrow."

"Thanks." She smiles, but it looks forced. "I'll let you know how it goes."

I'm tempted to ask her if she wants to commiserate later in the week, have a beer or seventeen shots of tequila, but then again, I probably don't have enough wow factor. The thought makes me yank the door open with a little too much force.

As I do, Melissa jumps back. "Oh. I wasn't sure you were still here. I was just coming to see if Angeline could come and take a look –"

"I'm here. Let's go." Angeline's voice is right behind me.

I turn, thinking she might shoot me a glance, maybe even a

half-hearted smile. Nada. She breezes by, taking a folder out of Melissa's hand and flipping it open as she walks. Melissa has the grace to look back at me, her expression a little sheepish, but I pretend not to see her as I stalk towards the front door.

Sarah calls out a *have a nice day*, but I don't wave in reply, and by the time I'm outside, my temper is almost as hot as the afternoon sun.

Fuck.

I'm annoyed at myself more than anything. I stopped by, assuming Angeline would be happy to see me. I'm not self-centered enough to think she owes me anything, including her time and attention. Hell, especially her time and attention.

But I assumed something that changed between us. Or maybe the problem is that I assumed there's an us at all.

Which proves the adage right. Only shit happens when you assume. This time the ass is definitely me.

Chapter Twenty-Seven
ANGELINE

I think people toss the phrase "week from hell" around too lightly. Like, I get saying it if you get really bad news – illness, death of a loved one, a personal tragedy of life-changing proportions – but the coffee maker crapping out? Not week-from-hell material. A board meeting where my fate is debated in front of me? Borderline enough to send me reaching for my Dad's gin stash on a Thursday night.

Which is where he finds me when he walks into the kitchen – bottle in hand and reaching for a glass.

"Whoa, since when do you drink gin instead of wine?" Dad asks. "Should I ask if you've had a bad day or just join you in a drink?"

"Join me so I don't have to drink alone." I hand him the glass and get another one out of the cupboard. "Is it too much to hope that we have tonic around here somewhere?"

"No tonic, but we have cranberry juice." I make a face and Dad says, "Trust me. Here."

He holds his hand out for the bottle and I give it to him, along with my glass when he extends his other hand. I watch him splash gin into the glass, followed by cranberry juice and ice. When he holds it out to me, I take it and bring it to my nose for a sniff before taking a small sip.

"Hey, this is okay," I say as I take another sip.

Dad sets the bottle of gin down on the counter and raises his glass to me. "Of course it is. Cheers."

He takes a drink and I have another swallow before he asks, "Want to tell me about it?"

I shrug. "The short story is that work is stressful, and as a result I haven't been very nice to, well, anyone."

Jack, in particular.

I feel way worse about the way I acted towards him than I've let myself admit. On the one hand, it's not my fault he came to my office and acted super sweet on a day when I was feeling epic levels of frazzled. On the other hand, it's totally my fault I took my bad mood out on him. I've texted him a couple times to apologize, but I know my attempts have been pretty paltry.

Dad eyes me over the rim of his glass. "Did being mean make you feel better?"

"I'm not five, Dad, so if you're gearing up for one of your 'it's nice to be nice' lectures, save it." Hearing my words makes me flinch, but Dad doesn't even blink and I let out a sigh of frustration. "Perfect example, sorry. It's not your fault I'm horrible."

"You're not horrible." Dad's tone is gentle. "You're having a bad week and lashing out. It's nothing new."

I raise an eyebrow. "Not really helping, Dad."

"Oh, Angeline, I love you more than anything. You know that, right?" Dad waits for me to nod before he continues. "But that you're defaulting to what you know isn't surprising."

"What the hell does that mean?" I may be thirty-two years old, but *hell* is about as strong as my language gets around my father, even when my blood is starting a slow boil.

"It means that you're nicer than you give yourself credit for until you're threatened, and then you scratch like a cat being forced into a bathtub. Do you remember what happened when Will teased you in front of your friends about cutting your own hair in sixth grade?" Dad takes a sip of his drink, but it doesn't quite hide his smile. "He might still be scarred from that."

I take a sip of my own drink and consider Dad's words instead of jabbing back at him. He doesn't have a malicious bone in his body – even about Will – so I know he's telling the truth as he sees it. The question is: is it the truth, full stop?

"A friend stopped by to surprise me at work the other day and I was stressed and took it out on him." Although I didn't so much take it out on him as ignored him, which was worse. Especially after everything that happened between us on Friday night. And the texts we exchanged while he was away.

"Did you apologize?" Dad asks.

"I texted, but he hasn't responded." Not that I'd expect him to, judging by the look on his face when he left my office.

"Texted?" Dad gives a *pshaw* sound that's basically his version of *bullshit*. This is still preferable to him picking up on the *he* part of that sentence.

"What? That's what people do these days, you know."

"I am aware. I don't live in a cave, after all. But you don't apologize via text." Dad says *text* like it's a curse word.

"You mean *you* don't. How would you apologize if you'd done something to make someone feel bad?" I cross my arms over my chest, then just as quickly uncross them. Eli used to call it my default defensive mode and he wasn't wrong.

Dad shrugs. "It depends on the person and what I did. If it was careless with what I said, I might write them a note, but if it did some real harm, I might take them flowers or ice cream, or flowers *and* ice cream if I was a first-class jerk."

No wonder Mom married him.

I think about bringing Jack flowers or ice cream and I don't think the reaction I'm imagining is the one I'm going for. I shake my head. "I'm not sure that would work in this case."

"Well, you find out what does work." Dad's tone has an edge of exasperation in it. "The thing is if you really want to apologize, you do it. End of story."

"It sounds easy when you put it that way." I give Dad a wry smile.

"Give me more specifics about him and I'll be happy to tell you what I'd do." Dad's eyes stay focused on his drink, which is the only way I know he's asking about Jack. In his very Dad way of not asking at all.

"Don't get excited, Dad. He's just a guy I…" I stop because I don't know how to finish that sentence, especially with the *just* in it. Jack's moved past the *just* stage, even if I can't put him in a different one yet.

"Is he one of those blind dates you've been on?" Dad asks.

I nod. "Yeah. Which means it doesn't take a rocket scientist to figure it out, but I'd really, really like you not to give me your opinion on him."

"Even if it's favorable?"

"Yes. I don't know what's happening yet. Maybe nothing because, as I said, I screwed up. But also because I need to know I can trust my own judgment and if you weigh in, good or bad, I've got that in the back of my head, you know?" I've only had a few sips of my drink, so I can't even blame the alcohol for the sudden stinging in my eyes.

Dad nods and his face is somber. "I don't think your judgment has ever been in question."

"Maybe not with you, Dad."

"I've always felt bad about the way the whole Eli situation played out, you know." Dad shuffles his feet like he's gearing up for a major conversation about this.

But I can't face that right now. Not nine months after the fact on the heels of a conversation about Jack, so I say, "I know.

Me too. But you think I need some kind of grand gesture to remedy the current situation?"

If Dad is surprised by the change in subject, he doesn't show it as he says, "Grand gestures are for grand things. I think you need *a* gesture."

I nod at the distinction and take another sip of my gin. Dad does the same and we stand in the kitchen in companionable silence until I say, "Thanks, Dad. You really are the best, you know."

"I am, aren't I?" Dad grins as I let loose a laugh. "Are you disagreeing with me, young lady?"

"I would never. I was just hoping to be able to tell you without it going to your head. Lost cause, I see." My smile is wide.

Dad grins, but his expression turns serious as he says, "You know you can come to me with anything, right?"

I slice my arm through the air, gesturing around the kitchen. "I'm thirty-two years old and living at home so I can pay off the last of my Manhattan debt. I think you've made that more than clear, Dad."

"I know, but your mother was always better at this stuff than me." Dad takes a sip of his drink. "She was the one you talked to."

Dad isn't often maudlin about Mom. But every once in a while, he says something that makes me realize how much he misses her. I cross the kitchen and put an arm around his waist. "I talked to Mom more because we were outnumbered and I had to have someone to commiserate with about how annoying it was to share the bathroom with Will and Theo."

"You did spend an awful lot of time in that bathroom." The corner of Dad's mouth turns up.

"I was a teenage girl. It's part of the job description." I grin. "Besides, it was also annoying, which is obviously part of the job description, too."

Dad laughs and the sound makes me laugh, too. Until he says, "Oh, sweetheart. You are something else."

My heart constricts at the word sweetheart because somehow that's become Jack's word. My eyes land on my phone on the counter across the room. I'm tempted to text him again, but I'm pretty sure Dad's onto something in suggesting I need to make a gesture.

I squeeze his waist and set my drink down on the counter, glad I've only had a few sips. "I don't mean to cut this short, but I think there's something I have to do."

Dad nods. "No problem. Should I wish you luck?"

"Maybe. Yes." For a second I consider backing out. I don't know if Jack will be alone, and what if he's not? We don't have any kind of agreement, but that doesn't mean I want to see him with another woman. Then I think about not seeing him at all and turn to Dad and say, "Actually, you can probably help. What kind of ice cream do you recommend?"

Chapter Twenty-Eight

ANGELINE

I stand outside Jack's front door and count to five as I squint up at his apartment, Sergio's veggie pizza in one hand and a pint of Ben and Jerry's Karamel Sutra melting on top. The setting sun reflects in the glass, making it impossible to see if any lights are on. I count to five again and glance around for a sign of his truck. It could be in the driveway behind the building. I half-hope he'll pull up to the curb to save me the agony of deciding whether or not to ring the buzzer. Even though I'm here, it doesn't mean I'm going to do it.

My finger hovers over the button and my hands feel clammy as I second and third-guess myself. Jack and I had one hot make-out session. Well, two if you count that first night weeks ago. He probably hasn't given me a thought since he walked out of my office two days ago.

I believe that like I believe in Santa Claus.

If he hadn't given me a second thought, he would have answered one of my texts. Stupid logic, but when one of them said *Warning: Your mother is in a bad mood today.* and it got no response, I knew. He also didn't answer the one that said *Sorry, it's been a stressful week.* Which was a half-ass apology on my part and I can't blame him for ignoring that one.

So who's to say he won't ignore me being here in person?

Oh God. Heat flushes across the back of my neck and my arm balancing the pizza box jumps up ten degrees. Five minutes more and I'll combust. I squeeze my eyes shut and push my finger to the buzzer. Part of me hopes I miss, but nope. I get it on the first try.

Jack's voice crackles through the speaker. "Yes?"

"Um, hi. It's Angeline." The pizza tips wildly as I shrug and I lurch to catch it. "Shit. Not you. I mean, I'm not saying that to you. I'm just...do you think I can come in?"

The door buzzes without Jack saying anything and I push it open with my hip. When I look up, Jack's standing on the second step from the top, a pair of cargo shorts low on his hips and a t-shirt in hand. His hair is damp and tousled and he's so clearly just out of the shower that I can still see water droplets on his chest. His incredibly well-defined chest that leads to even better abs. I haven't forgotten Jack's fabulous physique, as much as I've forced myself not to picture him naked because I've been so focused on work. Now that feels like a supreme waste.

I stop on the third stair because I need a little distance to get my words out. "I brought a peace offering."

Jack says nothing.

"My dad suggested flowers and ice cream, but I wasn't sure you're a flowers kind of guy, so I brought pizza and ice cream." I smile and it feels so forced it's ridiculous. "Sergio's veggie. It's still a little hot, but you can put it in the oven."

Jack still says nothing.

"I'm sorry I was a bitch when you stopped by *Pink*. I was flustered. And I didn't do a very good job of apologizing, but I'm trying to apologize now." I make myself stop talking, but I have to bite my tongue to do it.

Doesn't matter because there's still nothing from Jack.

"I'm willing to apologize profusely, but unless you say something soon, I'm going to assume you don't want to hear it and I'm going to leave and take the pizza with me." I glance down in hopes it hides the flush rising in my cheeks. "You can have the ice cream. It's a little melted, though."

Jack's lips turn up in a smile and it feels like such a victory I almost go weak in the knees and tumble backwards. "Is melted ice cream all you're offering, sweetheart?"

"Well, that and pizza. What you see is what you get, right?" I raise the pizza box in front of my chest like a half-ass salute.

"What if I said I didn't want the food?" Jack asks, his smile fading.

My heart sinks. "That's fine. I get it. I was a bitch and I don't expect anything. I just wanted to apologize."

I take a step backwards as Jack says, "I don't want the food or the apology. Although I appreciate both. I'd come down, but I'm not sure we'd ever leave the hallway if I did and my apartment is a lot more comfortable."

"You want me to come up?"

Jack's voice softens. "If you want to."

"I do. I do." I say it twice because I'm not sure whether the first time is just in my head, and my feet start to move up the stairs.

All I hear is my flip flops slapping on the wood. And the blood roaring in my head. I get one step away from Jack and he turns, heading into his apartment, before turning to wait for me right inside the door. My steps slow a little as I approach the threshold, but he reaches for the pizza box in my hands and tugs at my other arm as I give it over to him.

In one fluid motion, he sets the box down and pulls me inside his apartment, kicking the door shut. The next minute, his hands are in my hair, I'm backed up against the wall, and

Jack Reese is kissing me like he's a dying man and I'm his last breath. God, talk about weak in the knees.

Fact: Jack and I had sex the other night and he did not kiss me like this. Hell, I was almost married and have never been kissed like this.

Also fact: I'm the one who breaks away, my breath coming in short gasps. "I thought you were mad at me."

"I was." Jack's thumb grazes the skin behind my ear. "And then I realized I was being an asshole."

"But you didn't return any of my texts?" I furrow my brow at him and I hope it hides the fact that, life-changing kiss aside, his admission kind of niggles at me. And by kind of niggles, I mean it makes me wonder what part of realizing he was being a jerk meant Jack didn't think he should return my texts?

"I got your address from my mother. I was showering so I could come over and beg your forgiveness."

Jack's face is so earnest there's no way I don't believe him, but I still ask, "Were you really?"

"I even have an order in for a veggie pizza from Sergio's." He grins. "Great minds."

"You're serious?" I can't help how big my smile is, but then my brain catches up with his words and I ask, "Oh my God, what did you tell your mother when you asked for my address?"

Jack laughs. "I said I needed to return your bra."

The blood drains from my face. "Jack, she's my boss. You didn't."

"I didn't." He grins and pulls me to his chest. "I told her you'd left your wallet at Oh My Bagel and Chris asked if I could get it back to you."

"And she bought that?"

"She offered to bring it to you herself, but I didn't think you needed my mother darkening your doorstep."

"Definitely not. My father would die." I pretend to shudder, then squeeze my eyes shut with the realization of what I just said. "And shit, yes, before you can ask, I'm thirty-two years old and I live with my father. I was really broke when I moved back, and he was nice enough to offer..."

"Broke, I understand." Jack nods.

I wait a beat for him to say something else, but he doesn't and I let my shoulders drop. My voice holds a hint of a smile when I say, "So, let's get back to you begging my forgiveness. What was that going to entail, exactly?"

Jack grins at me and then yanks me by the hand. "It's way better if I show you, sweetheart."

Who am I to argue?

I laugh and follow Jack out of the kitchen and through his apartment. He turns and flashes one more grin at me as we cut through the living room, and I make a mental note to thank my father for his suggestion. He was right. This is way better than a text.

Chapter Twenty-Nine

JACK

*a*ngeline Sinclair in my bedroom was not how I pictured this night going, but I'm not about to look a gift horse. And granted, she's in my bedroom because it's the only room in the apartment with AC and it's approximately seven hundred degrees outside, but it's not a bad thing. Especially with her leaning against my headboard, pizza crust in hand, looking like she belongs there.

"Do you always eat your dinner in your bedroom?" she asks, a smile playing around her mouth.

I shake my head. "Usually I eat in the shop."

"Right. Because you keep your shop air conditioned, but not your house." Angeline's eyebrows go up and her smile widens.

"The wood responds better to a moderate temperature. The ideal temperature is about seventy degrees, with fifty to seventy percent humidity. Anything more and the wood can warp, any higher and −" I break off and shake my head. "Feel free to stop me anytime."

"Why? This is your passion and it shows." Angeline's smile changes and turns a little shy. "Keep going. I like it."

If she'd reached over and squeezed my balls, I don't think I'd feel half of what I feel right now hearing those words from her lips. Yet, I revert to type, wriggling my eyebrows as I say, "Do you now, sweetheart? Why don't you tell me what else you like?"

Angeline narrows her eyes because I swear she knows what I'm doing before I do. But goddamn, if it's not a punch to the gut when she says, "I like you, Jack. In case you aren't sure. I know I was a jerk when you stopped by. Sometimes I have a hard time compartmentalizing."

A remark about her using SAT words is on the tip of my tongue, but I think if I said it, she'd walk out of here forever, and I wouldn't blame her. So instead, I say, "I shouldn't have just stopped by expecting you to have time for me, and I'm sorry I got my ire up about it."

"Your ire?" Angeline laughs. "Wow, just when I think I've got a handle on you, you go and speak like an eighty-year-old man."

"You think you've got a handle on me, do you?" I grin and pick up the pizza box between us, setting it on the bedside table. "From over here, it looks like you're keeping your hands to yourself."

She glances at my hands. "Likewise."

This isn't like the other night when we didn't leave the couch. We're in my bedroom, on my bed, and I can't pretend I don't want Angeline again under me writhing and naked. "If I touch you, I'm not going to want to stop."

I don't mean to, but my words sound like a warning.

"Who's asking you to?"

I don't know who moves first, but when we meet in the middle of the bed, it's explosive. I yank her shirt from the waistband of her skirt and find the hot smooth skin of her back as her nails dig into my shoulders. I feel like I'm devouring her, but Angeline's hunger matches mine.

Her shirt is off and her tit is in my mouth when I ask, "What are you doing about your date tomorrow night?"

My timing is epic, but I have to ask.

Angeline pushes herself up on her elbows. "What do you mean?"

I kiss my way down her ribs to buy myself a second because I don't know what the fuck I'm doing right now. I let my tongue dart over her skin as I say, "I mean, are you still going?"

She freezes like someone shot her with a stun gun. "I have to, Jack."

Her voice is soft, but it doesn't make it any easier to hear. I let out a long, slow breath and nod, my chin resting on her stomach as I say, "I thought you were going to say that."

"It's my job, *Pink's* future, and everyone else's job. I can't not go." Her voice turns breathless as I move down and kiss her inner thigh. "I'm sorry. I wish I didn't have to."

"I know." I do. But goddamn it, if I don't hate the thought of it more than I hated it just a few days ago.

I let my fingers slide up her thighs and my mouth follows. I need to taste her. And, selfishly, I want to make her come so hard she forgets her own name. My tongue finds her center and she draws a sharp breath in. "Jack."

"Angeline." Her name comes out in a low growl.

"What are you doing?" She sounds breathless and I let my tongue flicker against her again.

And again.

"Finishing what I started." I taste her one more time and her fingers tighten in my hair. She gasps and that tiny sound is nearly my undoing. I want her. Not just now. Not just this.

I want all of her.

Chapter Thirty

ANGELINE

"Your hair is doing a weird thing in the back. Let me fix it." Melissa holds her hand out for my brush and I give it to her. I need to leave in six minutes to meet Ian, tonight's date, and I'm not ready in any way. Mentally, my head is still in the throes of last night, and physically, too, if I let my mind go *there*. But even if I don't, the fact that I got ready for work in fifteen minutes this morning and didn't bring a change of clothes for tonight's date does not a date look make.

I watch in the mirror as Melissa twists my hair into a high top knot. "My neck looks gawky with my hair up like that."

"Your neck looks fine. Besides, it's ninety degrees out. In an hour you'll be happy to have your hair up. An outdoor movie is a great idea, but it becomes a little less great on the hottest day of the year."

Melissa's eyes are focused on my hair, not my face, so she doesn't see me grimace. "Do I have to go? I don't want to. You know that, right?"

"But you're going to and it will be fine." Melissa meets my eyes in the mirror. "Jack knows the deal."

"He knows I'm stuck doing this series." But he doesn't like it. Which he didn't – and wouldn't – say, but what guy on the planet doesn't want a little bit of reciprocation when things get that hot and heavy? He either is the issue or he has an issue, and I'm pretty sure in Jack's case it's the latter.

I haven't told Melissa all the details from last night, but she knows enough to say, "He knows you weren't counting on someone like him coming along."

"It's only one more week." In the grand scheme of things, a week is nothing. So why does it feel so long? "And it's not like I can't see Jack in the meantime, right?"

"You tell me. What did you two decide?" Melissa asks as she takes a hair band from around her wrist.

We didn't. We fell asleep tangled up in each other and when I woke up this morning – twenty minutes before I was supposed to be at the office – there wasn't any time to talk. Aloud, I say, "I'm not sure, honestly."

"Well, Jack's a realist. He knows what's riding on this series." Melissa pulls a few strands of hair loose to frame my face and turns me around by the shoulders to face her. "There. Better. Speaking of being a realist, you need to go."

"I know. Are you sure you don't want to come with me?" My tone is hopeful.

"This is supposed to be a date, remember? I know your heart's not in it, but you have to stay long enough to have something to write about." Melissa grins. "Who knows? Maybe he'll be another Lowell and you can bail."

"Honestly, if he's another Lowell, my faith in men is going to take a major blow." I lean into the mirror to scrape my fingernail in the corner of my eye to get rid of a smudge of eyeliner.

"I thought Jack was turning you into a believer?" Melissa raises an eyebrow.

"A Belieber, did you say? I think his taste is more Justin

Timberlake than Justin Bieber, if you want to know the truth, but I'll ask him."

Melissa rolls her eyes. "Fine. Be that way. But for the record, I see your avoidance tactics, and if you didn't have to leave I'd never let you get away with that."

Dodging Melissa's pressing questions is one thing. Getting to Highland Park on a Friday night when there's a film on is almost enough to make me think I'd prefer to be trapped in the ladies' room with Melissa after all. Traffic is a nightmare, the AC in my little Honda is wheezing in this heat, and I haven't even tried to find parking yet.

Then there's the Jack part of this whole thing. All day, I've been trying not to think about him, but a guy walks by who has such similar hair I do a double take, and I remember how his curls felt tangled in my fingers last night. Then I think of how he put the brakes on sharp and fast. Not that he left me hanging, but he left himself with a major case of blue balls. And let's be honest, it's not like I didn't offer to help him with that situation.

I squirm in my seat and give my head a firm shake, meeting my eyes in the rearview mirror. Getting hot and bothered before this blind date isn't going to do me any good. Neither is feeling guilty. Which is the name I finally give to the feeling that's been plaguing me all day. I feel guilty I'm going out with someone who's not Jack, even though we've had a grand total of one real date.

One real, perfect date.

Followed by one real, perfect night. Then last night, which was almost perfect.

I let out a heavy sigh and thwack my palm lightly on the steering wheel. Then I take a deep breath in, holding it for a silent count of ten before letting it go. Guilt isn't going to save my job, but neither is Jack. Melissa's right – I need to stay out with Ian long enough to have something to write about and then I can make an excuse to leave. I already know where I plan to end up.

The thought buoys me enough to focus on the cars lining the street. Finding a parking spot here is challenging at the best of times, but suddenly a car turns on its blinker and noses out. I wave wildly for the driver to ease out in front of me, and in three smooth turns, I'm in the space. Parallel parking at its finest, thank you, New York City. I lean back against the seat and revel in the air conditioning because now, due to my stellar parking spot, I'm actually early.

The thought makes me smile and it feels like the first genuine smile I've had all day. I can do this. It's no different than going out with a colleague. Well, except that I don't work with this guy and he wrote in to nominate himself.

We've had a few of those, but they've always been hard and fast nos. Like the guy who wrote in and said he'd bring me over to his mother's for dinner, and then maybe afterwards we could watch repeats of *The Great Bake Off*. Then there was a guy who said he'd applied to *The Bachelor* over seventy times because he couldn't imagine anything better than having twenty hot women to choose from. The worst one was probably the guy whose date suggestion was a concert at the University of Rochester and dinner afterwards – in the dining hall of his dorm.

Ian, though, seems normal – a mechanical engineer with a house in Webster, his write-in was funny and self-deprecating. Judging by the photo he sent, he's not bad looking either. Not Lowell handsome, but that's not a bad thing. And he's picked a super low-key date – an outdoor showing of *Ferris Beuller's Day Off*. Under different circumstances I would probably be looking forward to this. And I never look forward to dates.

Another consequence of my relationship with Eli Quinn.

I let out a sigh. Damn Eli. He's weighing on my mind today like a tumor.

Hint: it's not because of Ian.

But Jack isn't Eli, is he? And I'm not the same person I was then either. Am I?

The fact that I can't answer either of those questions with a resounding no is something I need to think about. Later.

I close my eyes and bang my head gently against the seat. Jack. Eli. Eli. Jack. Their faces spin in my head until I feel seasick. Then I open my eyes, take a deep breath in, and check my teeth for lipstick in the rearview mirror before swinging open my car door. I can't afford to sit here and ruminate over Eli and Jack. It's time to get to work.

Chapter Thirty-One

ANGELINE

*I*an is...cute. And nice. Five-ten or so, blond hair, blue eyes, great hands. I know it's a weird thing to notice about a guy, but his hands give the impression he's strong and sure, and I find that attractive.

He's also super attentive. I think there's such a thing as too attentive and he's veering in that direction, but it feels mean to fault him for it.

"The movie starts in about fifteen minutes, which is enough time to hit the food trucks. Are you more of tacos-and-beer or a steak-burger-and-Cabernet kind of girl?" Ian kneels next to me as I sit down on the striped picnic blanket he's brought.

"Definitely tacos and a beer. Do you want me to come help carry?"

"No, no worries. Stay here and keep our spot. I spent a few summers as a cater waiter, so I should be able to manage." Ian flashes me a grin. He has nice teeth. "Any taco preferences?"

"Anything's fine, but no three-alarm salsa." I think of Jack sneaking the jalapenos onto our pizza and I add, "I don't handle super spicy food very well."

Ian laughs and stands. "Noted. Tacos with mild salsa coming up."

I smile back at him and he turns to weave his way through the crowd towards the food trucks lining the park. It's crowded and Ian has to do a lot of jostling around blankets, legs, and feet. I watch him for a few minutes – he has a good butt, too. By blind date standards, so far he's a ten out of ten. Why I don't feel enthusiastic – or much of anything at all– is definitely not a reflection on Ian.

I shoot off a quick text to Melissa. *BD #3 isn't a dud. The dud is me! I'm not doing a very good job of faking it.*

Melissa answers immediately. *Pretend you're at one of those awful awards dinners you have to write up sometimes. Same principle.*

I nod at my phone. *Good point. How much longer?*

Melissa sends me back the eye roll emoji and I grin. I give a furtive glance around for Ian and pull up Jack's Instagram feed – which is mostly pieces of furniture and photos of completed jobs – when I feel someone sit down beside me on the blanket. I hastily put my phone facedown on the blanket before turning and... "Jack? What are you doing here?"

"Hi." There's a playfulness in his expression. "How's it going?"

"Fine?" I swivel my head around to see if Ian's nearby, but just as quickly turn my attention back to Jack. "What are you doing here?"

"I wanted to see how your date was going."

"Um, fine, but I don't really think this is appropriate."

"Eh, appropriate a-shope-mi-ate." Jack shrugs.

"I'm serious, Jack. You can't be here."

"I'm serious, too." Jack's tone is resolute. "I know you're doing your job right now, but I hate it. I hate knowing you're out with somebody else who's going to want to kiss you goodnight. I hate knowing that you're out with someone else, period."

I furrow my brow. "We talked about this. There's a lot on the line here and I can't – won't – just bail. You not liking this doesn't change the fact that it's literally my job right now."

"Is a little creative writing off the table?" Jack asks. "I mean, what if you ditched like you did with Lowell and made stuff up for this one?"

He didn't really say that, did he? Judging by the look on his face, he not only said it, he meant it. "Have you ever heard of journalistic integrity? Believe it or not, it's a thing."

"Even for a feature like the 'Blind Date Diaries'?" Jack's mouth snaps shut like he wants to take those words back the minute they're out of his mouth, but it's too late.

They rattle in my head like an elephant in a cage.

"You know what? Ian's going to be back in a few minutes with our food and you're in his spot." My voice is ice cold.

"I'm sorry. What I said was insensitive and out of line. I'm sorry."

"Great. Thank you. It was." I cross my arms over my chest like that will somehow hide my irritation.

"I'm sorry. I said I was sorry and I'll say it again. That was a stupid thing for me say." Frustration seeps into his tone, which doesn't do him any favors.

"Yes. But did you mean it, Jack? People have a funny way of letting the truth slip out despite their best intentions." For how hot it is, I manage to keep my expression Arctic.

Jack's, though, is what I can only describe as pure Jack – a little pissed off, a little dismissive, and arrogant as hell. "I thought we'd gotten past this."

"What do you mean by this?"

"This thing where you assume I'm an asshole regardless of what I say or do."

I narrow my gaze because if he's going to turn this around and blame me... "I don't assume you're an asshole."

"But you assume I meant to belittle your work." He shrugs and pushes himself to his knees. "Same thing, sweetheart."

"I assume you spoke carelessly, but you also showed up here with your own agenda and zero consideration for me. That actually might be worse." I bite my lip. Hard. "I need you to go before Ian gets back."

Jack springs off the balls of his feet and says, "Fine. Consider me gone. You have a great time tonight."

He takes a step away, and I half-expect him to turn around and apologize. But he thinks he already did that, doesn't he?

I push myself to my feet, stumbling a little on my wedge heels. I want to chase after Jack and yank his arm so hard it comes out of the socket, but I stand frozen because I know it wouldn't end there. I'd yell and cause a scene, and someone would figure out who I am. No doubt there'd be a video.

I'd implode the "Blind Date Diaries" all on my own, and my future along with it.

I swallow hard and smooth down my maxi skirt before sinking back down to the blanket. Where I finally let myself hear the thought that's been ricocheting around in my brain. Jack never asked me how I felt. Not once. It was all about him. Him, him, him.

Maybe Jack and Eli are cut from the same cloth after all. I bite the inside of my lip so hard I taste blood and tears spring to my eyes at the unexpected sting. At least that's what I tell myself. Because there's no way I'm going to tear up over Jack Reese.

No. F-ing. Way.

Chapter Thirty-Two

JACK

*T*alk about a major fuck up on my part. If I were trying to get a reaction from Angeline, this wouldn't be it. What the hell was I thinking would happen? I'd tell her I hated the thought of her out with other guys and she'd say *Yep. Sure. Whatever you want.* Like she owes me anything?

I haven't been this twisted up over a woman since Emma Blake my freshman year of college, and that was because she was trying to make my roommate jealous. Angeline's doing her job and I'm treating it like a personal affront. Way to get the girl, Reese.

I drive for ten minutes, berating myself the whole time. I don't even know where I'm going, except it sure as hell isn't home because my sheets still smell like Angeline's perfume and that's not going to do me any good. My truck feels like it's on autopilot when I turn down Park Avenue and start trawling for a parking space. Maybe a drink or three will solve something. It sure as hell can't hurt.

I end up in the Old Toad, which is funny in a not-funny-at-all way because this is where everything started with Angeline. It's way too crowded for my current mood, but judging by the bottles of amber liquid lining the shelves behind the bar, they have plenty of liquor, so it will do just fine after all. It's not like I have to talk to anyone.

I've just ordered a Jack Daniels on the rocks when I feel a hand clap my shoulder. I turn, scowl in place, to find Theo, Angeline's brother, saying, "Hey, Jack. Good to see you."

He reaches out to shake my hand and I take it because I'm not a total dick, and if he's talking to me, he obviously hasn't heard from Angeline. Not that she'd go texting her brother to tell him I'm an asshole, but they seem close, so he's going to hear it sooner or later. May as well hear it from me. "Good to see you, too. I should probably warn you, I fucked things up with your sister and you talking to me right now probably goes against some sort of sibling code."

Theo nods. "Okay, thanks for the heads up. Was it fatal?"

I blow out a long breath. "Probably."

"Shit. I'm sorry. I thought you two were, you know." Theo doesn't make any attempt to expand on that, but he doesn't have to.

"Yeah. We were." I take a swallow of JD so I don't give in to the urge to go into the dirty details.

"Well, if it helps, Ang has a history of being pretty forgiving," Theo says.

"You mean like her entire relationship with Eli?" A guy comes up beside Theo and sticks out his hand. He's taller than Theo, but the family resemblance is unmistakable. "Will Sinclair. Nice to meet you."

"Jack Reese. Same." I shake his hand and his grip in mine is a little too firm. Great, he's one of those guys.

"Has Ang told you about Eli?" Will asks.

If I were a decent guy, I'd say no and offer a hard pass. But since we've already established I'm not a decent guy, I say, "Not really. She's pretty close-lipped about her past."

"Not without reason, dude." A look passes over Theo's face

as he says this like he either has gas or this conversation is making him queasy.

"Hey, no harm, no foul. No one gets through their twenties without scars." It's a clear invitation to drop the whole subject, which makes me feel like I've redeemed myself a little. No one *has* to continue this line of conversation.

Although if I had to, I'd bet on Will running with it.

As if on cue, he says, "Eli was an asshole. He had a thing on the side for months while they were engaged."

"Shit." I don't know what else to say so I take another swallow of my drink. At this rate, no way in hell I'm driving home tonight.

"That sucks, obviously, but it was more than that. Eli had a big personality and a big career, and what he wanted, he got. He wanted Ang and he was going to make sure he kept her." Theo takes a long swallow of his own drink. "She was in line for a big promotion at work and Eli threw her chances out the window by telling her boss that he was up for a promotion, too, and when he got it, they'd be moving to the west coast."

"Was he?" I raise my eyebrows over the rim of my glass.

"Don't know. If he was, he never mentioned it to Ang. The first she heard of it was when she asked her boss why she'd been passed over for a job she was overly qualified for."

"Shit." I say it with more feeling this time.

"She called him on it and he asked her to marry him," says Will.

"She said yes." It's a statement, not a question, but that doesn't mean I don't have at least a thousand of those.

"It was what she thought she wanted." Theo shrugs. "Sometimes it's hard to see the forest through the trees and by that point Eli had done a damn good job of making her believe what he wanted was the most important thing in her life."

Fuck.

Theo's words are a punch to the throat and I shake my head. "That's fucked up, but it explains a lot."

"That's not even the half of it," says Will.

I hold up my hand. "Angeline is already pissed at me and I doubt she'd appreciate me getting the full low down on her past from her brothers. If she ever speaks to me again, it's for her to explain."

"Whatever you did, it can't have been that bad." says Will.

"It can." I set my glass down on the bar, even though there's still some liquor in it. "I think I pretty much just pulled an Eli on her."

Theo lets out a low whistle. "Bad move, even without her history."

"No shit." My lips twist in a grimace. "Any hints for how to redeem myself?"

"Go big or go home, man," says Will with a chuckle.

"Seriously. Skywriting an apology over the whole of greater Rochester would not be out of order," adds Theo.

"Skywriting, huh? Shit." I nod slowly, but my mind races.

Skywriting, I can't do. But there might be something I can.

Chapter Thirty-Three

ANGELINE

*D*ad left to go golfing an hour ago and I've been sitting here staring at my computer screen trying to think of what to write about last night's date with Ian. All I have so far is: *It was fine*. Which will get a worse reception with Victoria than if I'd suggested she try L'Oréal. She might even throw something at me.

The problem is, it *was* fine. Ian was nice. The movie was good. Yes, the night was humid, but I'm not going to complain about that. I'm not going to complain about anything that happened on the date itself because it was fine.

Not fine? Jack showing up like he had every right to be there. And yes, I'm still mad. Quite possibly furious. I know that's why I can't think of anything to write. Every time I start, I see his smug expression and hear his tone filled with expectation, and I feel my blood boil all over again. If Will were here, he'd tell me to go for a run and do something constructive with my frustration. Since he's not, I've got a bag of Fritos open beside my laptop and I am working my way through it.

I've just popped another one in my mouth when the kitchen door rattles behind me and Will comes in carrying cardboard takeout containers, followed by Theo bearing a container filled with four venti Starbucks cups. I glance at the clock – it's 9:30 on a Saturday morning. Usually Will is working at this time; Saturday is a big day in the personal training business. I turn my attention to him first, saying, "Hey. What are you doing here?"

"I had a cancelation, so we brought breakfast." Will sets the containers down on the table and I smell pancakes. And bacon.

I narrow my eyes because if Mr. Fitness bringing pancakes and bacon isn't suspect, I don't know what is. "Thanks. I think." I turn to Theo and say, "Dad's not here. He got a golfing invitation he couldn't refuse. One of the guys is going to splurge for a golf cart, apparently."

Theo nods and hands me a coffee. "Nice day for it."

He slides one of the food containers over to me and I close my laptop. It's not like I was getting anything done anyway. I open the container, breathing deep to inhale the bacony syrup goodness. My eyelids flutter and I open them in time to catch an expression on Will's face that can only mean one thing. This breakfast is his penance.

"What did you do?" My tone is sharp. "I wasn't born yesterday and I've seen that expression plenty. So, what did you do?"

They exchange another look and Will says, "We ran into Jack last night."

My breathing quickens. "Okay? And?"

"Will told him about Eli," says Theo.

"Way to throw me under the bus, dude." Will throws his hands up.

"What? You did." Theo crosses his arms over his chest.

"I think you filled in plenty of blanks yourself." Will's hands move to his hips, clenched into fists.

Battle lines are drawn between Will and Theo, but I'm having none of it. "Enough. What did you tell him?"

Theo gives me a bare bones version of what was said, ending

with, "He wasn't digging, I swear, and honestly, Ang, I really thought you would have told him."

"Why? What makes you think I want to talk about Eli with anyone?"

"Maybe not anyone. But a guy you're involved with? Yeah, I thought you'd have told him about the guy who fucked you over six ways to Sunday." Theo rolls his eyes, which makes me mad.

Well, madder, and I'm looking for a target for my anger. "First, who said Jack and I were involved? Second of all, what business is it of yours? And third —"

"Are you involved?" Will asks. "If not, let's start there because Jack seems to feel you are."

"I don't think that concerns you." I glare and push my chair back so I can get a fork. I'm either going to eat pancakes with it or stab one of my brothers. At the minute, it could go either way.

"You can't run from this Eli thing forever," says Theo.

I whirl around faster than a ballerina in the Nutcracker. "There is no Eli thing. I left New York almost nine months ago, and my relationship with Eli is over."

"Exactly," says Will. "You left New York nine months ago and have never looked back. Don't you think that's weird?"

"How is it weird? I found out my fiancé was cheating on me three months before our wedding, I called it off, and moved back to my childhood home. That isn't great for your morale, in case you're wondering. Most of the people I thought were my friends claimed they suspected, which is awful, but it also means they weren't great friends in the first place, and that still stings. I spent almost two years of my life with a guy who was lying to me, but was going to go through with our wedding anyway, and friends who were older versions of the bitchy girls I hung out with in high school but with better clothes and shinier hair. And you're wondering why I don't look back?" My voice has risen at least two octaves while I've been ranting. "Would you look back if you were me?"

"All I'm saying is that it's pretty critical info not to share with someone," says Will.

Before I can explode again, Theo adds, "Jack said he pulled an Eli on you last night, but that doesn't mean he's the same kind of guy."

"He said that?" My eyes widen. "How much did you tell him?"

"Not that much," says Will. "He said you deserved to be able to tell him yourself."

"Obviously." I clench my teeth together.

"Or not," says Theo. He gives Will a pointed look. "How you talk or don't talk about Eli is your prerogative. But if you're looking for Eli in every guy you meet, I'm here to tell you, you're not going to find him."

"Thanks for the insight. I realize that," I say.

"Do you?" Theo's tone is soft. "Jack made a mistake last night, but he's not a bad guy."

"How do you know, Theo? Do you really know him that well?"

He shakes his head. "No, but I know you. You're not the same person you were in New York. You're smarter and kinder and a hell of a lot more open in all the ways that count. You'd also never let yourself fall for another guy like Eli."

"You're right. I wouldn't. But who said I'm falling for anyone, period?"

"No one. But you didn't say you weren't either." Will grins. "Are you going to eat that bacon? Because I need some protein before I meet Lacey."

"Lacey? Is she a client or a booty call?" My tone is snide, but Will deserves it.

"Uncalled for." Will reaches for the bacon in my container. "Can I have it?"

I glare at him. "After you answer my question."

He gets a wicked gleam in his eye. "Do you want to play that game, sis? Because I'm pretty sure you've left a pretty big question on the table yourself."

I know when I've been defeated and let out a long breath before I push the container towards him. "Fine. Have my damn bacon."

As Will picks it up between his thumb and forefinger, Theo asks, "So what are you going to do about Jack?"

"I don't know." I point to the table. "But I've got Fritos, coffee, and pancakes, so I'll figure something out, right?"

Theo's phone buzzes and Will reaches for another piece of bacon. My guess is they'll both be gone in five minutes, leaving me here with our conversation on a loop in my head, wondering if some of my anger is because my brothers are right and I've fallen for Jack Reese.

Chapter Thirty-Four

ANGELINE

"What about this guy?" Melissa shoves her laptop across the table. "He's cute."

I skim the bio. Political science professor at a local college. Divorced with a daughter.

"Nope. He has a kid." I shake my head. "I'm not comfortable with that."

"You don't have to marry him. You're, like, going to dinner and a movie or something." Melissa yanks her laptop back. "There's always the sneaker guy."

I make a face. "When the most interesting thing about you is that you own fifty-six different types of sneakers, you might want to reconsider your life choices."

"What about the guy whose nomination came in a couple weeks ago? The lawyer? Brian something?" Melissa peers at her laptop screen as she scrolls. "He was cute. No kids. No weird collections or hobbies."

"He's a trust and estate lawyer. Boring with a capital *B*." I pick up last week's copy of *Pink* from the stack on the chair beside me and look longingly out the window. It's a perfect summer day. We've commandeered the conference room for this conversation, but I can't help wishing I'd taken Melissa's suggestion and gone across the street to Oh My Bagel and snagged an outside table. Of course, Melissa and I both know the reason I nixed it, but she's been kind enough not to mention it so far. "We need someone who will bring in the big bucks. Advertising has picked up, but I don't think we're out of the woods yet."

"Haven't Victoria and Mike shared the numbers with you?" Melissa looks up.

"They have, but it doesn't feel like enough to me." Especially not the way Victoria keeps stressing how I need to really "bring it" for my final date. She didn't specify what *it* actually is, but the fact that she's using slang sounds alarm bells loud and clear. "Maybe we should pick the sneaker king after all."

Melissa scrolls down quickly and clicks on his profile, turning her laptop screen so I can see. Steve Marshall, twenty-eight, retail manager at Footlocker. Aside from the sneaker collection thing, he seems okay. I'm just about to open my mouth to say that when Patrick walks in without knocking and says, "Are you really looking at Steve-o, man? What happened to letting the readers nominate your dates?"

"We did that with Lowell and Ian," I say. "But for the last one we need something great and I don't think we can trust the readers on this one."

"Uh, uh. That's not how this works." Patrick plucks the magazine from my fingertips and flicks through the pages. "Where's this week's issue?"

"No idea. I looked in Mike's office, but he's not here and all I can find is last week's." I shrug. "Doesn't matter. All of the nominations come through online anyway, so we pretty much have the pool we're working with at this point."

"So you haven't seen this week's issue at all?" Patrick's voice becomes a little more urgent.

"No, but as I said, it's no big deal."

"But as the editor shouldn't you see it? That's a really stupid process if you don't even see the finished product." Patrick's voice rises a little more.

I furrow my brow because I can count on one hand the number of times I've seen Mr. Chillax anything other than calm and cool. "I'm sure I will. Why? Is there a problem?"

"No, but you need to see it, man." Patrick shoves a hand through his hair. "Stay right here. I'm going to hunt one down."

"Sure. No worries." I glance at Melissa and she shrugs back at me.

"And don't decide anything yet." Patrick turns at the door. "You're not emailing the guy today, right?"

"We're just doing reconnaissance," says Melissa. "You know the readers pick Ang's dates."

She winks, but it's lost on Patrick, who's already striding out of the conference room. I turn to Melissa. "What was that about?"

"No idea. I haven't seen this week's issue either." She wriggles her eyebrows. "But obviously there's something in it you need to see. Maybe Ian has written an impassioned plea for a second chance?"

I bark out a laugh. "I doubt it. We had a nice time, but I didn't get the feeling it was unforgettable for him."

It definitely wasn't for me. After Will and Theo left on Saturday, I spent another couple hours staring at my computer screen, trying to think of synonyms for nice. I even broke out the thesaurus, but I know my write-up was only a little better than lukewarm.

Honestly, the only write-up that hasn't been lukewarm has been Jack's. He's also the only date I've given a second and a third thought to. In fact, most of my staring at the computer screen on Saturday was because I was thinking about Jack.

"Have you heard from him?" Melissa asks.

I glance up. Did I mention Jack's name out loud? I'm closer to losing it than I thought. "Who?"

"Ian." Melissa grins. "Who did you think I was asking about?"

"No one."

My reply comes out too fast and Melissa's eyes narrow so much she looks like she's squinting in the sun. "Okaaay. Have you heard from him, then?"

"Not really." I haven't told Melissa about Jack showing up on Friday night.

"Last time I checked, that was a yes or no question. What does not really mean?"

"It means I don't want to talk about it." That's a lie. I do want to talk about it. Preferably over a bottle of Malbec with a bag of Fritos. Or two. The office conference room is no place to discuss how confused I am about all things Jack Reese. On the one hand, I'm still furious with him. On the other, I suspect he didn't mean to come across the way he did. If I'm being generous and giving him the benefit of the doubt, maybe he thought he was making a grand gesture. Like me with the pizza, but with more balls.

How the hell did he think that was going to go? Did he really think I'd ditch Ian and walk off into the sunset with him? How shitty would that have been? And for Jack to expect it is even shittier. Which is me right back to furious.

"You're scaring me a little over here, you know." Melissa's voice rings through my reverie. When I look up, she's got a small grin on her face. "I can't tell if you're pissed off, confused, or both, but I do know I wouldn't want to be on the receiving end of any of it."

"You wouldn't." I shake my head. "You want to grab a drink after work?"

"I'm supposed to go to spin class, but I could be convinced

to skip it for Rosalie's and Taco Tuesday." Melissa wriggles her eyebrows. "And the full scoop, of course."

I'm just about to agree when Patrick bursts back into the conference room, waving this week's issue of Pink. "Found it. Mike says this one is going fast."

Patrick's got a sly smile on his face and I hold my hand out for the magazine. He doesn't hand it over. I furrow my brow. "What's the deal? You can't wait for me to see this and now you won't give it to me?"

"I'm just wondering if I need to preface it at all." Patrick says.

"Okay, now you're making me nervous. Preface what, exactly?" I exchange a look with Melissa, but judging by the blank look on her face, she doesn't know any more than I do.

"Ah, never mind. I think blind is better, man." Patrick hands the magazine over to me and I take it like it might explode in my hands.

I flip quickly through the pages until I get to the center spread. On the left-facing page is my write-up of Friday night's date with Ian, but it's the right-facing page that makes me gasp.

I look up at Patrick. "You knew this was in here?"

He nods and Melissa says, "What? Let me see."

I drop the magazine onto the table and Melissa lets out a low whistle. "Whoa."

Whoa, indeed.

Staring up at us is a photo of Jack Reese with the words *I'm sorry* superimposed over his face. There are a lot of other words on the page too, but my eyes dart over them, catching only snippets. Until I land on a paragraph that says *Angeline would be the first one to say I don't get to come here and ask for favors. She's right. But I'm asking because I'm not sure I'll get a second chance otherwise. Nominate me for her last blind date. I know it's not blind. I know it's not the way this is supposed to work. But I also know Angeline wants to do right by this series. By her readers. By her Pink Ladies. And I want to do right by her. More than anything.*

Holy. Guacamole.

I'm too stunned to even swear. "Did you or Erin help him write this?"

"No way, man. This was all Jack. I just did the layout and shit."

The *layout and shit* is great, but it's got nothing on the words. I'm still staring at the page when Melissa asks softly, "So, are you going to go out with him?"

I don't know. This is a capital *G* Gesture. There's no walking away from this pretending it's not a big deal. I nod slowly and say, "I think it's up to the readers."

"Are you kidding? Ravi's worried the server's going to crash." Patrick scoffs.

"Because people are nominating Jack as my date?" My pulse flutters in my neck. And my stomach. And the backs of my knees.

"Like it's the Mega Millions." Patrick laughs.

I wonder for a minute if I'm having a heart attack. Or a panic attack. It could be either. Possibly both.

"I guess you're going out with Jack Reese then," says Melissa.

I nod. That's all I can do because that pulse in my throat is ricocheting off my teeth now and I'm not sure if it's with nerves or anticipation.

Chapter Thirty-Five

JACK

hris texted two hours ago asking to borrow a drill, but I've got the electric sander going when he arrives at my shop on Tuesday afternoon, so I see him before I hear him. He's got two white sandwich bags in one hand and a copy of *Pink* in the other, which causes my stomach to somersault. I'm hungry and queasy at the same time, which is how I've felt for the past two days. This time hunger wins.

I turn off the sander as Chris hands me a bag. "Thanks, dude. What's today's special?"

"For you, Rye Can't We Beef Friends – roast beef on rye with cheddar cheese, horseradish mayo, and fried onions. I've got a Beef You To It, which is roast beef, lettuce, and tomato." Chris grins. "I can't handle the horseradish. Kills me every time."

My mouth waters and I unwrap the sandwich in the foil. It's still hot and I sink my teeth into it with a moan. I'm chewing when I say, "Thanks, dude. This is awesome."

Chris grins, but then his expression turns serious. I know what's coming, and before I can swallow, he says, "So, some spread you've got in *Pink* today."

"Yeah." I'm not really sure what else to say.

"Has Angeline seen it yet?"

"I don't know. If she has, I haven't heard from her." It's after two o'clock, so I'm pretty sure she has, but I keep telling myself something could have happened.

"What do you think she'll say?" Chris asks, taking another bite of his sandwich.

"No idea." This is the absolute truth and I taste the horse-radish in my throat for a second time.

"What if you don't hear from her?"

"You mean, like, she blows it off completely?" Damn that twist in my gut. Like I haven't thought that ten thousand times. To Chris, I shrug. "Maybe the readers will take pity on me."

"Are you sure it's pity you want?"

"Empathy, then." I want them to put Angeline and me together for the final date and I don't care how it happens. Except... "You know what? If she's not into it, it's fine. I'm not going to beat a dead horse."

"I'm sure the horse would appreciate that." Chris grins, but it fades as he says, "How would it make you feel?"

"Seriously? Are you my therapist now?" I growl like a pissed off pit bull.

"Just asking." Chris is either oblivious to my tone or he doesn't care.

"It's pretty fucking obvious, don't you think?"

Chris shrugs. "It's not obvious until you say it."

"I'd feel like shit." Possibly worse.

"Why?" Chris takes another bite of his sandwich. Like we're discussing the fucking Yankees and not the woman I'm falling –

"I'm done with the psychoanalysis, dude. Sorry. I put the drill by the door for you. Don't break it." I go to flip the switch of the sander back on.

But I'm not fast enough. "The article is great, but unless you tell her how you feel, you're still at square one. Say she agrees to go out with you for the final date. Then what?"

"Christ. What do you not understand about the word done?" The hand not holding my sandwich is squeezed into such a tight fist I'm surprised my knuckles don't pop.

"If you can't admit it to yourself, there's no way in hell you're going to win her over." Chris turns back towards the door, calling over his shoulder, "Just saying."

"No one asked you," I say to his retreating back. "Just saying."

"Isn't that the beauty of it?" Chris grabs the drill and pulls the door. "Later, dude. Let me know when you hear from her."

It's a good thing the only object within reach is a hammer and throwing it would break the glass in the door. I'm smarter than that, but if there was no window, you can bet your ass it would be following Chris's path. I'm so pissed I don't even look at the caller ID on my phone when it rings, yanking it from my pocket, and answering with a sharp, "What?"

"Darling? Is that any way to greet your mother?"

Fuck. Me. I let out a long breath. "Mom."

"I haven't seen you much recently." Mom's tone is easy.

Mine isn't. "Yeah, sorry. I've been busy."

"I see." I imagine her pursing her lips on the other end of the phone. "I saw your page in *Pink* today."

Of course she did. "Yeah, um, about that..."

"How did you get that through editorial? Actually, whose idea was it? It's brilliant." There's a smile in her voice.

I'm so confused I almost forget I'm even mad. "Brilliant? What do you mean?"

"I mean, darling, that we've never had so much web traffic. IT can barely keep up and Ravi said the server crashed briefly." Mom sounds gleeful. "I don't know why we didn't think of it sooner."

"Think of what?" I'm not dumb, but I'm going to need her to spell this out for me. Just to be sure.

"Giving the date's perspective. It's Angeline's diary, but of course she's not going on these dates by herself." She still sounds like she's smiling. "And readers love someone to root for."

"Do they?" What I really want to ask is *are they rooting for me?* But I don't.

"Of course they do." Mom lowers her voice a little. "And you've obviously been a reader favorite all along since they're coming back in droves to nominate you."

That answers that question then. "Well, good. I guess?"

"Angeline must be pleased. Have you checked in with her yet?"

"Is she pleased?"

"Well, I assume so. Didn't you two —?" Mom stops abruptly. I imagine her mouth forming a little red *O*. "She wasn't the one to push it through editorial."

It's not a question, but I'm compelled to answer anyway. "No. I kind of bribed Patrick."

One of the benefits of *Pink* having a bare bones staff. I'd never have gotten away with this in a bigger magazine with actual processes in place.

"Oh, Jack." Mom's voice softens.

This is way worse than Chris goading me. "Don't, Mom. Just don't."

"Well, rest assured, the readers are on your side. You'll win this week's nomination by a landslide."

"Good to know."

"I'll be in the office in about forty minutes and I'll check in with Angeline." Mom hesitates, but not long enough for me to speak. "Do you want me to get a read on her for you?"

"No thanks, Mom. It's nice of you to offer."

"It was bold, Jack. What you did. If I can see that, Angeline will, too."

Bold? Try desperate.

Aloud, I say, "Thanks. We'll see."

"Well, I'm rooting for you, and so is most of Rochester." I'm half-waiting for an admonishment. Something along the lines of *don't blow it*, which is what I'd expect. Instead, Mom says, "Love always wins, Jack."

Cynical me wants to bark out a laugh, but I can't do it. Instead my voice is low when I say, "Thanks. I hope so, Mom. I really do."

I hang up and roll the word around on my tongue.

Love.

That's what this is. Chris knows it. My mom knows it. Even the part of me that can't quite say it out loud knows it. But none of that matters if Angeline doesn't know it too.

Chapter Thirty-Six

ANGELINE

*V*ictoria calls a Wednesday afternoon staff meeting, which in itself is unusual, but not totally unprecedented. What is unprecedented is that she's told me nothing about it. When I try to ask, she just gives me this closemouthed smile and shakes her head. So, if I'm sitting here on the edge of my seat tapping both my pen and my heel, well...it's understandable, right?

"Thank you all for giving me a few minutes today," Victoria says to start. "I want to start by congratulating you on the success of our new series these past few weeks. Despite being a little slow out of the gate, the *"Blind Date Diaries"* has reengaged readers in a way we haven't seen since *Pink's* early days."

"Advertising is up, finally," adds Mike. "We've expanded our advertising base, which is great."

"That was the overall goal, of course. And now we're at the last date." Victoria pauses and looks around the room, but her eyes don't land on me. Meanwhile, my heel might drill through the carpet in a minute. "Obviously, the final date will be Jack Reese. I think we'd have a mutiny on our hands if we tried to send Angeline out with anyone else."

Victoria pauses to allow people to laugh. I try but fail. I do, however, manage a grimace that might pass for a smile. Because readers are clamoring for Jack and me to go out Friday night. But the man himself? Not. A. Word.

"I think we need to mix it up and I have two ideas. One is that we get Jack and Angeline to live tweet their date." Victoria holds up her forefinger.

"Hashtag *TBDD?*"

"No." I'm halfway out of my chair before she can say any more. Over my dead body am I live tweeting anything. But then I look around the table and see the amusement on everyone's face – well, everyone except Melissa, who looks as horrified I do – and sit back down, perching on the edge of my chair as I say, "Victoria, have you ever been on a date where both people are glued to their phones? There's nothing good about that. And trust me, I would know."

I give her a pointed look and this time Melissa laughs. Victoria rolls her eyes, but says, "Fine, point taken. Then we get Jack to write up a rebuttal."

"A rebuttal?" I know what the word means, but not in this context.

Victoria waves her hand like she's swatting away a gnat. "You know, his perspective on your date. They can appear side-by-side in the final write-up of the "Blind Date Diaries"."

I have no reason to object, other than the obvious. I have no idea what Jack will actually write. Before I can speak, Melissa says, "Isn't that risky? What if Jack and Angeline's versions don't match up?"

Victoria smiles, showing her teeth this time. "What if they don't?"

Is that what she's hoping?

"This series is supposed to be romantic, not a he-said, she-said," Melissa says. I seriously owe her a pizza later. And a bottle of wine.

Victoria's smile fades and her eyes turn laser sharp. "This series is supposed to be a reader magnet. Romance is secondary."

Oh God. I've wondered if Victoria knew about Jack's plea in *Pink* and decided it was a firm no, but now I'm not so sure. For all I know, she put him up to it. The thought makes my heart sink.

"Has Jack agreed to this?" Patrick asks from the other side of the table.

Victoria purses her lips. "No, but I didn't agree to him having a page in this week's issue either. I'll consider it like for like."

Jack took out that page on his own. Victoria had nothing to do with it. Like a bouncy ball, my heart slams into my throat.

"If Jack is amenable, maybe a side-by-side would work? The "Not-So-Blind-Date Diaries"?" Melissa suggests. I nod in agreement. Not so much because I think it's a great idea, but because it's the lesser of God knows how many evils and I don't want to hear another suggestion from Victoria.

"Fantastic. Will you sort that out with him, Angeline?" Victoria asks, giving me a perfunctory glance before saying, "Patrick, I'm going to need to coordinate with you on some sort of graphics to wrap this all up."

"Sure. We can roll right into "The Wedding Diaries" as the next feature?" Patrick shoots me a grin across the table.

"There would be worse things. Are any of you getting married?" Victoria glances around the table for a show of hands. "Well, never say never. We'll sort something out. For now, ladies and gentlemen, let's finish this series off with a bang. And, Angeline, if I could speak to you for a moment."

"Um, sure." I can't very well say no, but I feel like I'm being called to the principal's office for making out with her son behind the bleachers. It's not a great feeling.

Victoria waits until everyone leaves and the door closes,

leaving us alone in the conference room. She doesn't say anything at first, which doesn't make me any less nervous. Finally, she clears her throat and says, "What are your intentions towards my son?"

"What?" My eyes widen and I feel my spine stiffen. "I'm not sure I know what you mean."

"Are you stringing him along? Do you care for him? Is it something in between?"

There's no good way to answer this question, so I stutter. "Umm."

Of course, Victoria's having none of it. "I know you, Angeline. I'm sure you've thought about your feelings for Jack or lack thereof."

I've done nothing but think about my feelings for Jack. Especially knowing he's my date Friday night. But that doesn't mean I want to talk about them with his mother. Aloud, I say, "I'm sorry, I'm not happy to discuss that with you." It's surprisingly easy to hold Victoria's gaze. "My feelings for Jack are irrelevant to *Pink*."

"My question isn't related to *Pink*." Victoria's eyebrows disappear underneath her heavy bangs.

"Yes, I understand that." I clench my back teeth together hard so I won't say anything else.

Victoria levels her gaze at me. It's the same one she uses when she's talking revenue reports with Mike and me, and usually it starts one of us sputtering. But not today. Although she gives me plenty of opportunity, waiting a full minute before she says, "Well. I do hope you both have a lovely time."

She swings open the conference room door and strides out, calling Patrick's name as she goes. I wait until she's rounded the corner to let my jaw unclench and let out the breath I've been holding. *What are your intentions towards my son?* What kind of question is that? And more importantly, if I knew the answer, why would I bother waiting for Friday night to come around? Right now, it's buying me time. And I need every second.

Chapter Thirty-Seven

ANGELINE

*A*side from clothes, shoes, and cosmetics, I didn't bring much from my Manhattan life back to Rochester. A cute set of plates from Fish's Eddy with the New York City skyline lining the edge. A pile of autographed books from the time *Lush* sent me to cover the Romance Writers of America conference. And a box of cards and trinkets from my life with Eli.

I know, I know. Ruminating on my relationship with him is the equivalent of offering a hungry Rottweiler a steak. On my bare ass. But we were happy once and I felt like I'd want to remember that someday.

Turns out that someday is now. I'm sitting on my bed with my shoebox of Eli mementos strewn around me, staring at the first Valentine card I got from him. We'd been dating for a few weeks and he'd sent a box of Godiva chocolates to my office with a card that reads *I'll pick you up at 6 tonight. Pack a bag. Clothing optional.*

God, I was so excited. And even more so when we ended up on a helicopter to the Hamptons. My first helicopter ride. My first trip to the Hamptons. My first weekend away with Eli.

When we pulled up to the house where we were staying for the weekend – compliments of his boss – it started snowing and I had to pinch myself, it was all so magical.

I feel a small smile on my lips and dig further into the box. There's the keychain of the Empire State Building from when we first exchanged keys to our apartments. And the *Today's Specials* menu card I slipped into my purse from dinner at the River Café when Eli asked me to move in with him. Sifting through pieces of paper, my fingers land on something slick and smooth.

I steel myself because I know what it is before I look. I don't have many printed photographs – thank you, digital technology – but there'd been a photo booth at a wedding we'd gone to and Eli and I had hammed it up for the camera. I look down and my heart clenches like someone's wrapping their fingers around it and squeezing. Hard.

My hair is sleek and straight, my skin just the right shade of expensive fake tan. I let myself marvel at the fact that since moving back to Rochester, the need for bronzer hasn't crossed my mind once. Then my eyes slide over to Eli, in his dark blue suit and pink wedding tie, his head thrown back laughing. His smile rivals my own and we look So. Damn. Happy.

It was the first summer. Before his company Christmas party when his partner got handsy and Eli told me to deal with it. Before our disastrous trip Upstate to visit my family when Eli spent the whole weekend on his phone "working." Before last summer when he asked me to marry him. Before I said yes, despite my reservations.

God, was I really that naïve?

I throw the box off my bed, watching as the contents rain on my rug like sad confetti. I'm not even sure who I'm angry with – myself, Eli, fucking Rachel – but I am sure of one thing.

My fingers fly over the numbers on my phone before I can

second-guess myself. Eli answers on the second ring. "This is Eli Quinn."

My breath catches. His voice is low and deep. There's no noise in the background, which probably means he's still in the office. It's only 9pm.

"Hello?" A trace of irritation edges into his tone.

It's what I need to propel me to speak. "Eli."

"Angeline?" He sounds surprised.

I'm surprised, too. How the hell can he tell it's me from just two syllables?

"I have a question."

Surprise morphs into wariness. "Okay?"

Silence thrums down the line. Eli and I had one blow out when I discovered the whole Rachel thing. Not because I had incredible self-restraint, but because he didn't try to explain or justify or win, and that broke my heart more than his sexting ever could.

"Why did you ask me to marry you?"

"What?" I can picture Eli furrowing his brow. "What kind of question is that?"

"You didn't love me. So why did you ask me to marry you?" My voice is brittle around the edges and I take a deep breath in through my nose to steady myself. For good measure, I dig my fingernails into my palm as well.

More silence, then Eli says softly, "I wanted to love you, Ang. I thought if I couldn't make it work with you, of all people, there was no hope for me. I was trying to be a better man."

"You failed." I swallow down the lump forming in my throat. I will not cry over this man again.

"I know." Eli pauses and his voice drops. "I'm sorry. There are a lot of things I regret, but what I did to you is my biggest regret by far."

"That doesn't redeem you." I flex my fingers and examine the crescent moon marks on my palm.

"I know."

I wait for him to say more, but he doesn't. I think of all the things I could say to him, but I don't. Instead, I listen to his breath on the other end of the phone for two minutes as I watch the red second hand of the clock on the bedside table make its slow spin around the numbers.

When it passes the three a second time I say, "Goodbye, Eli."

"Ang —" Eli starts.

I shake my head and when I speak this time, my voice is stronger. Sure. "Goodbye, Eli."

I press end on my phone without waiting for his reply and close my eyes for two deep breaths. When I open them, I scoop up the items from my shoebox and toss them inside before shoving it back under my bed.

My room feels stuffy. When I yank open the door I smell toast. My stomach rumbles in response and I trot down the stairs to see Theo in the kitchen, bent over the toaster oven.

He turns to me and says, "Hey, I'm making cheesy toast. You want some?"

"Yes, please." I nod. "Don't you have food at your own house?"

"No." Theo laughs. "I thought I heard you on the phone. Talking to anyone in particular?"

I'm pretty sure he's digging, but I just smile and say, "Nope. Just someone I used to know."

Then I laugh because the crazy thing is, I mean it. For the first time, I mean it.

Chapter Thirty-Eight

JACK

I stare at the single red rose on the passenger seat of Chris's Jeep as I pull up to the curb in front of Angeline's place. The rose felt like a good idea three hours ago. Now it feels somewhere between cheap and just plain cheesy. Like I should have gone for a dozen and in any other color rather than red. Then there's the whole do-I-bring-it-to-the-door dilemma. If her dad answers, I'll be anxious anyway. The last parents I met were Kat's and we were an actual couple. I'm not even sure Angeline wants to go out with me tonight or if she's doing it for *Pink*.

Which is why I'm picking her up at her house in the first place. Obviously, we're past the blind date stage and I couldn't stomach the thought of meeting her in a public place. Or worse, arranging to meet her in a public place and her not showing. Her one-word response to my text – *okay* – saying I'd pick her up at 7:30 wasn't exactly encouraging.

I shoot one more glance at the rose. Fuck it. It stays here. Then I hop out of the driver's seat, slamming the door behind me, and set up the driveway. There are two cars in the driveway and my heart starts a steady thumping in my chest because only one of them is Angeline's. Shit.

By the time I'm standing at the front door, I'd be surprised if the neighbors can't hear my blood pounding. And my palms are sweaty to boot. Jesus. I wipe them on my khaki shorts and press the doorbell.

Of course, her father answers the door. Or at least I assume the tall, broad, balding man behind the screen is her father. He smiles and says, "Jack, I presume?"

"Yes, sir." My response is automatic. I may be shit at a lot of things, but no one will ever say my mother didn't drill my manners into me.

He pushes the screen door open. "Matt Sinclair. Come on in. Angeline should be down in a few minutes."

"Thank you." I step over the threshold into the cool foyer and it feels like home. Not my home because my mother's foyer is white and filled with more mirrors than a fun house. But this is welcoming. There's a table with a lamp and a large bowl of keys on it, a few pairs of shoes by the side, and one of those photo frames filled with old family photographs. I take a step and peer at the photo in the bottom left. It's Angeline and her two brothers dripping wet, standing in one of those plastic kiddie pools and eating ice cream. I smile and say, "Great photos."

"Those were the days," Matt says. "Those three kids played in that pool until we had to duct tape up the sides."

"That sounds like a lot of fun." My summer swimming pool was at the country club down the street, which was great. But I feel a stab of nostalgia for the kind of childhood I imagine Angeline had, nonetheless.

"You have brothers and sisters?" Matt asks.

I shake my head. "No, sir."

Matt raises an eyebrow. "You don't have to call me sir. I'm

not going to quiz you on your intentions and remind you to have my daughter back by midnight."

I know he's joking and trying to set me at ease, but I can't help responding, "My intentions are good. I've made some mistakes, but I'm hoping Angeline will at least hear me out tonight."

"Are you?" Her voice is soft behind me and I whirl around.

She looks fucking amazing. Let's get that out of the way first. She's wearing a strappy black sundress that shows off her cleavage, flat sandals, and carrying a small black bag in her hand. Her hair is long and wavy around her face and her mouth is turned up in a shy smile.

"Wow." I let out a long breath. "You look terrific."

Matt clears his throat behind me. "Um, I'm going to get out of here. I'm meeting Lou and the guys down at the Sports Page to watch the game. You kids have fun."

"Bye, Dad. Have fun." Angeline waves, but her eyes stay on mine.

I don't say anything because suddenly my heart is jackhammering in my head again. I lift a hand in a wave as Matt brushes by me, pulling the door closed behind him.

Meaning it's just me and Angeline in the foyer. I clear my throat twice before I croak out, "So."

"So." Angeline's eyes are wide and filled with expectation.

But I'll be damned if I know for what. "You're going to have to give me a little more to work with, sweetheart."

"You're the one who took out a full page in *Pink* to be my date tonight. I assumed you had something to say." Angeline turns like she's going to head back upstairs.

Before I can stop myself, I reach for her wrist. "I needed you to agree to be my date tonight, and I wanted to do it fair and square. I know how important this is to you."

"My brothers told me they gave you the dirty details on Eli." Angeline's expression doesn't change, but she gently extracts herself from my grip. "I'm not doing that again. I'm not going out with someone who manipulates me into thinking I'm less-than because of my job, how much money I do or don't make, how thin I am or not, whether I top up my fake tan −"

"Whoa, sweetheart. I don't care about any of that."

"You care about winning and the reason you're here tonight is because you won the blind date fair and square." Angeline offers a tiny shrug.

"I brought you a rose." I blurt it out and Angeline looks at me like I'm speaking Chinese, but I continue. "You know how on those stupid shows they always end with a rose ceremony? I know technically it would be you handing out a rose, but if it were the other way around, I'd have handed it to you on day one."

"Day one?" Angeline's eyebrows go up.

"I've had a thing for you for quite a while, sweetheart." I try to grin but can't. Not with Angeline looking at me that way.

"You've had a funny way of showing it." Angeline pauses. "Until lately, anyway."

"You kind of seemed to hate me." Understatement. "Not exactly encouraging."

"Did you ask your mother to be a part of the 'Blind Date Diaries'?"

Rather than ask me out yourself.

Angeline doesn't say it, but it hangs in the air like she did.

"No. That was just luck." I shake my head. "She asked me and I was hoping it would be an opportunity."

"And the night at the Old Toad?"

"That was luck too, although part of me wishes it never happened."

"Why?"

"Because I like you looking me in the eye after I've had my hands and mouth all over you." My cock nods in agreement.

"I like that, too." Angeline swallows and her gaze heats up as she says, "Almost as much as I like your hands and mouth all over me."

Fuck. Me.

"Am I supposed to be taking that as an invitation, sweetheart?" God help me if I'm reading this wrong. "Because I made a reservation at Rocco and I'm second-guessing that right now."

"Good." She licks her lips. "I don't want to go to Rocco."

"Fair enough." But staying here when Matt could walk back in the door any minute is not an option.

"Do you have a plan B?"

I do and amen that I don't have my head completely up my ass. Aloud, I say, "What are you thinking?"

"Somewhere we can be alone would be nice, I think." She raises her eyebrows at me in a silent question.

"I know just the place." I take her hand and her fingers wrap around mine.

Chapter Thirty-Nine
ANGELINE

I assume we're going to Jack's apartment, but then he
leads me to the Jeep and hands me the rose – cheesy,
but it makes me smile like a kid with a packet of Starburst.
Then he holds out a black knit scarf and says, "Do you
trust me?"

Loaded question.

Still, I nod. "Um, yes?"

"Then you'll let me tie this over your eyes?"

"Um, no. Why?"

"Putting the blind in blind date, sweetheart." Jack grins.

"Five minutes ago you said you made a reservation at
Rocco."

"If that's what you chose, that's where we would have gone."
Jack holds the scarf closer. "You said you wanted Plan B, and
this is Plan B."

"Blindfolding me is plan B?" It's not even that I mind so
much, but it means Jack is in the driver's seat on this in every
possible way.

"It's part of Plan B." Jack's smile widens. "It's up to you if
the blindfold comes back out later."

I laugh. "Okay, fine. Go ahead."

He wraps it loosely over my eyes, but doesn't make any real physical contact until he guides me into the Jeep, and even then, he just settles me in my seat and quickly closes the door. After I hear his door slam and the engine purr to life, I say, "How long will it take to get to where we're going?"

"Twenty minutes or so." Jack reverses and starts off at a crawl down my street.

We don't talk at first because I imagine him navigating Friday night Park Avenue traffic, so I wait until we pick up some speed before asking the question that's been playing on repeat since he mentioned it in my dad's foyer. "So, how long is quite a while exactly?"

Jack's laugh fills the car. "Remember the day we met?"

I scrunch my nose up. "That day at your mother's luncheon?"

"Yep." Jack laughs again. "I'd say it started then."

"Why? You were so rude that day." I wince a little. "And I was such a bitch."

"You were a little reserved." I roll my eyes under the scarf, but it's lost on Jack because he can't see. "At first, I just wanted to rile you up."

"How very sixth grade of you."

"Not one of my finer moments. It took me about a minute to realize you give as good as you get because not only are you beautiful, you're smart as hell. Then I just wanted to get to know you, but the only time you'd speak to me was when we had these verbal sparring matches."

"Thus, a pattern was born." I shake my head. "I thought you hated me, you know."

"So you've said." Jack pauses as he makes a turn, then says, "Now it's my turn."

"Your turn for what?" My tone is wary because I think I know what he's going to ask.

"That night in the Old Toad? What was that about?"

Bingo. Guessed it in one.

That night feels like a long time ago. Especially on the heels of my conversation with Eli the other night. My words come out slowly when I say, "I wanted to hook up, but I didn't like you, so you were no threat to me."

"We've hooked up since then." Jack stops like he's going to say more but doesn't.

"It's different now. Somewhere along the line I discovered I like you." I pause and wish I could pull the blindfold down to see Jack's expression. "Which makes you a much bigger threat, to be honest."

"I never want you to feel threatened, sweetheart." Jack's voice is soft but serious.

"I'm not talking about a physical threat, Jack." My own voice turns a little breathy and I wonder for a second if we'd be having this conversation sans blindfold. Somehow, I doubt it, which is the only reason the next words come out of my mouth. "Your mother asked me what my intentions were towards you, you know."

"Holy shit. She did not." Jack's voice, by contrast, is firm. And more than a little appalled.

"She did." I smile a little. "I told her I wouldn't discuss it with her."

"Good." I hear the smile in Jack's tone. "Do I dare ask if you want to discuss it with me since you brought it up?"

"I think I'd rather see you when I answer that question."

As if on command, Jack makes another turn and slows down as the tires crunch on gravel. He doesn't speak but eases the car to a stop. The next thing I hear is the door slam and Jack comes around to my side and opens the door. His hands are gentle as he unties the scarf and pulls it away from my face.

I blink against the light and then gasp. The sun is setting

over Lake Ontario in front of me. To the right is a small cottage with a big deck on the lake. "Where are we?"

"Plan B." Jack reaches for my hand. "Come on."

I follow as Jack fishes keys from his pocket. When he opens the front door, I gasp because the cottage is one big room with a wall of windows facing the lake. A huge bed sits at one end and a small kitchenette at the other. In between is a big denim sofa and a wooden trunk doubling as a coffee table, complete with an ice bucket and two glasses set up. I spot a Blue Moon label through the melting ice.

"You must have been pretty confident I'd go with Plan B." I squeeze Jack's hand.

"Not even a little. Just hopeful, sweetheart. I pulled in a favor from a client who rents this place out." Jack laughs and squeezes my hand in return. "There's food in the fridge for later, but what do you say to grabbing a beer and watching the sunset?"

I turn towards Jack and place my hand on his chest. He's so solid. So here. So real. "What do you say about grabbing a beer and not watching the sunset?"

"I say I'm all for it. Tell me what you want to do instead."

There are times when actions speak louder than words and this is one of them. I move my hand down Jack's chest and reach for his zipper.

Chapter Forty

ANGELINE

I wake up on Sunday morning to the sun streaming in the windows and Jack naked at the other end of the cottage, making coffee. I take a minute to appreciate the view – I can't remember why I ever thought he wasn't good-looking – before calling out, "Good morning, sunshine. Is one of those going to be for me?"

Jack grins. "Of course. Although we're going to have to leave here if we want any serious food. The only thing left is a stale doughnut."

"Well, that's sad." I stick my lower lip out in a pout. "Unfortunately, we're going to have to leave regardless of the food situation. We have a he-said, she-said to write."

Jack clangs a spoon around in a mug and brings one to me, setting it down on the side table before walking around the foot of the bed and crawling back in. "Oh, don't worry. I am aware. Have you thought about what you're going to write?"

I thread my bare legs through Jack's under the quilt. "Well, I thought about mentioning the ticklish spot on your hip, but that might border on TMI."

Jack's hand finds my ass. "Really? Because I was going to

write about how you go crazy when I pinch your nipple as you're about to come."

"I'm not sure I need *Pink* readers to know that." I rest my hand on Jack's stomach.

"You know what I think they need to know?" Jack asks, pulling back to put some distance between us.

I frown in protest. "What?"

"That this blind date was the best thing to ever happen to me." Jack's expression is so serious it scares me a little because we've done a lot of talking – and not talking – this weekend, but we haven't talked much about feelings.

Which means I have a choice to make. Right here. I can either jump into this conversation with both feet or I can skirt around it. I move my hand up to his chest and feel his heart beating faster than normal. That decides it for me.

"This blind date was the best thing to ever happen to me, too." I swallow. "You know I'm probably going to fall for you, right?"

"Going to, sweetheart?" Jack grins. "Come on. You need to catch up."

"Catch up with what?"

"Me. I fell for you over that first pizza." Jack's grin is easy.

"You mean the pizza you snuck jalapenos on?" I try to muster up a scowl but end up giggling instead.

"Hey, if that's the worst I've got to offer, you're getting off light."

My smile fades. "I know. You forget, I've been there, done that."

"I haven't forgotten." Jack's smile fades as well. "I can't promise to never hurt you, but I promise to never hurt you intentionally."

"I know." Jack isn't Eli. If this weekend has done anything, it's solidified the differences between them. And the differences in me when I'm with them.

"And." Jack holds a finger over my lips. "If I do hurt you, I solemnly swear I'll make it up to you, tenfold."

"Likewise." I kiss his finger.

"I'm going to work on getting AC installed in my place and getting rid of the shitty window unit."

"What?" I furrow my brow. "I mean, great idea, but are you really thinking about home improvements right now?"

"Well, I can't ask you to move in until I've got that sorted out." Jack grins.

"Move in?" My eyes widen. "Isn't that kind of fast?"

"Nah. Consider it an open invitation." Jack's grin widens. "Whenever you're ready, sweetheart."

I search his blue eyes for a sign of uncertainty, but there is none. There's no pressure either. "I'm not ready yet. You know that, right?"

"Next week, next year, it's cool." His hand grips my hip. "I'm not going anywhere. I've had a schoolboy crush on you for months, and spending time with you has only turned it into something real."

"I still can't believe I was so blind to that." I let my hand wander up Jack's chest.

"Maybe that's the real reason why this thing is called the 'Blind Date Diaries'?" Jack laughs.

My whole body stiffens. "Oh my God, Jack. Your mother."

I can't articulate anything more, but I don't have to.

"What about her?" Jack laughs.

He laughs!

"She's my boss and you're her son." I mean, obviously, but my brain seems to have short-circuited on this.

"She thinks you're amazing."

"As her employee. As her son's girlfriend?" I shake my head. "I'm not so sure."

"My mother is the one who forced us together in the first place." Jack's smile is easy. "Maybe she knew that left to my own devices I wouldn't get my head out of my ass and I'd lose you to an Ian or a Lowell."

"Never a Lowell." I make a face. "Besides, you said she didn't know you liked me."

"She didn't. But who knows? Maybe she was playing matchmaker?"

That thought is even more disconcerting.

"Do you think so?"

"I don't know." Jack shrugs. "I don't care because it got us here."

True that. I would have never seen past my dislike of Jack unless we were forced together.

"I still don't want to tell her."

"So don't." Jack grins. "It's going to be pretty clear from our write up how this has all played out, sweetheart."

"Why? What are you going to write?" I try to look stern, but my big grin kind of ruins it.

"Nope. You're going to have to wait and see just like everybody else." Jack pulls me closer and his lips graze my shoulder.

"That's disappointing." I stick my lower lip out in a pout. "I don't want to be like everybody else."

His lips move to my neck. "Oh, trust me. You're not."

I laugh as Jack's mouth lands on mine. Our kiss is all teeth at first, but when his tongue meets mine, my smile melts into desire, and all thoughts of Victoria, *Pink*, and the "Blind Date Diaries" fade away.

Chapter Forty-One

THE "BLIND DATE DIARIES"

He Said

I owe you all.

Thank you to every single person who voted for me to go out with Angeline on her final not-so-blind date.

It was amazing. She's amazing. I'm the luckiest guy in Greater Rochester that this gorgeous woman has given me a second (or is it a third?) chance.

I'm going to do everything in my power to make her happy. Make that happier with lunch from Oh My Bagel today. Word is that Angeline likes a Brie My Baby, but I'm going to go for a Love The Way You Rye to mix it up a little.

And yes, in case you're wondering this is a shameless plug for the best bagel shop I know. Because not only are Chris's sandwich names guaranteed to make you wish you were half as clever, but the man himself is pretty clever, too. He knew about my feelings for Angeline and wouldn't let me bail just because it was hard. When you find a friend like that, keep a hold of them, even when you want to throw a hammer at their head.

And when you find a woman like Angeline, do everything you can to keep a hold of her, too.

See you at one, sweetheart. Hope you're hungry.

Chapter Forty-Two

THE "BLIND DATE DIARIES

She Said

*P*ink Ladies (and gentlemen) – Oh my! What can I say about my final date? Yes, it was amazing. Yes, you knew exactly what you were doing sending me out with Jack again. I am truly beyond grateful.

Pre-date effort: 10 out of 10. I have this dress from my NYC days that makes me feel like a super model when I wear it. The spaghetti straps show off my shoulders, the neckline is super flattering (hello, cleavage), and it's fitted enough to give me a good figure, but I can still eat a meal and not look four months pregnant afterwards. Also, it looks better with flats than heels, so double win. It was the only choice for my date, especially since I didn't have any clue what we were doing.

Nerves: 11 out of 10 – Oh my gosh, you guys. I heard the doorbell ring and my hands were shaking worse than if I'd had sixteen shots of espresso.

Date location: 10 out of 10 – I'm going to be coy about the location. Sorry, not sorry. But suffice it to say, there was food. And wine. And sunsets on the lake. Yes, you read that right. Sunsets, plural.

First impression: 10 out of 10 – I mean, seriously. Have you SEEN this man?

Disclaimer #1 – I didn't always realize Jack was good-looking.

Disclaimer #2 - I do now.

Swoon moment #1: *He brought me a rose. A rose!*

Swoon moment #2: *He blindfolded me en route to our date location. Unnerving, but talk about enhancing all your other senses!*

Swoon moment #3: *Donuts. A dozen of them.*

Swoon moment #4: *Um, all of them?*

The end: *the "Blind Date Diaries" is over, it's true. I won't be going on anymore blind dates, but I see plenty of dates in my future. And maybe the next installment you'll be reading here is the "Living Together Diaries". Or maybe not because it doesn't quite have the same ring to it. But it's in the works regardless, so you never know. Watch this space.*

Chapter Forty-Three

EPILOGUE

"*D*oes this dress look too short?" I tug on the hem like that will somehow make it longer and take a step backwards to study my reflection in the full-length mirror. "I swear it fit better in the store."

Jack turns from where he's tying his tie and rakes his gaze down my body, shaking his head slowly. "It looks great to me."

"But is it engagement-announcement great?" My palms feel clammy just saying the words. "I mean, you know your mother's planning a speech."

"And? If you don't want her to say anything, I'll put the kibosh on it right now." Jack gives his tie a final yank and crosses our bedroom floor.

Yes, *our* bedroom.

After our shaky start, Jack and I progressed quickly. I moved in with him right after Thanksgiving and we got engaged in March at the same cabin where we spent the weekend of our second date. We've kept our relationship quiet as far as *Pink* is concerned, but Victoria's having her May Day garden party this afternoon and she wants to congratulate us publicly. She also wants me to consider chronicling my wedding planning as a summer series, and I'm pretty sure this is her way of goading me into it.

So far, I've avoided giving her a definite answer.

I look up at Jack as he puts his hands on my hips and pulls me to him. "There's no harm in letting your mom tell everyone we're engaged. She can shout it from the rooftops as far as I'm concerned. I'm just worried she's going to tell everyone that there's going to be a "Wedding Diaries" coming soon."

"We'll tell her we're eloping to Vegas and getting married by an Elvis impersonator." Jack grins. "That will solve the problem."

"Will it though?" I can't help grinning in reply as I imagine Victoria's expression. "She might find that strangely appealing. I know I do."

Jack's smile fades. "If that's what you want, sweetheart, say the word and we're on the next plane. The most important thing to me is marrying you, not how we actually do it."

"See? This is why I love you." I kiss the corner of Jack's mouth. "I think you honestly mean that."

"I'm serious." Jack's expression mirrors his tone. "You said the wedding stuff was going to be important to you. You know, after Eli. But if you've changed your mind..."

Once upon a time, invoking memories of Eli would have made me cringe. Now, I nod in agreement. The wedding Eli and I had planned was extravagant, but shallow – much like Eli, himself. I want mine and Jack's wedding to be elegant and relaxed - but, most of all, genuine.

"Do you think the fact that I haven't actually started planning it yet is a sign I've changed my mind?" I ask the question even though I know my lack of planning has more to do with lack of time than anything else. Things at *Pink* have been insane and my free time has been taken up with enjoying Jack. In every sense of the word. The thing is, I don't see any of that changing anytime soon.

"Or it's a sign you've changed your mind about getting married in general?" Jack raises an eyebrow.

"I haven't." I stare at him until he meets my gaze. "I'd marry you right now without a second thought."

"We could, you know," Jack says. "I mean, technically, we'd have to get the marriage license today and wait twenty-four hours, but by this time tomorrow it could be a done deal."

"Ummm, what about your mom's party?" This is the question I ask instead of the one about how Jack knows there's a twenty-four-hour waiting period to get married after applying for a marriage license. I mean *I* know it, but only because the requirements are the same in Manhattan as they are in Rochester.

"We'll be a little late." Jack shrugs. "I'll tell her I was having trouble tying my tie. She'll buy it, don't worry."

Victoria will buy that. Jack's right.

"Ooo-kay. And then what? We'll just go back tomorrow and get married?" My stomach flip flops as I say the m-word, but I think it's in anticipation.

"Sure. Or, you know, next week if you're busy?" Jack gives me a lazy grin. "I cleared my schedule for today, so I'm supposed to be in Webster tomorrow to meet a client. But I could probably put him off."

"Do you think so?" I laugh. "That's generous of you."

"You say the word, sweetheart, and I'm wherever you want me to be." Jack pauses. "Including the city clerk's office."

"Would we, like, invite people?" My dad would hate not being there, and I can only imagine what Victoria would say if her only son got married without her.

"Either way." Jack leans back and looks at me. "I see your mind spinning through all of the possible scenarios. Before you get too far, remember we don't have to do it this way. I just said we could. I would."

"I know." Jack's right. My head is spinning like a Tilt-a-

Whirl. My Dad. Victoria. My brothers. Never mind who gets married on a Friday? Is that the story I want to tell our kids someday? I open my mouth to say no, but as I do disappointment thuds hard in my chest. Those earlier butterflies in my stomach suddenly feel like slugs.

"Sweetheart, come on." Jack leans down and kisses me softly. "Let's get ready to go. The earlier we arrive, the earlier we can leave."

"I think we should do it." My words come out in a whoosh.

"You think we should get our marriage license and get married tomorrow?" Jack says slowly. "Or you think we should go the party?"

"All three." I feel a laugh bubble in my chest. "I think we should detour to get our marriage license on the way to the party. Then tomorrow we can get married."

"Are you sure? I mean, yes. Obviously, I'm one hundred percent on board with this plan. But it's not the real wedding I thought you wanted." Jack's hand cups my cheek.

"Are you trying to change my mind?" I raise an eyebrow at him.

"I'm just making sure, sweetheart." Jack's gaze is so earnest I have to swallow down a sudden lump in my throat.

"I'm sure. I want this. I want you to be my forever." I feel my eyes prick and I swallow hard again. "Starting now."

Jack spends a long minute looking into my eyes, then he kisses me. His lips meet mine and his tongue sweeps into my mouth like he's done a thousand times before. But it feels different this time. This time it feels like a promise.

I feel Jack's arousal pressing against my stomach when he breaks away, saying, "We need to stop there, sweetheart, or we'll never leave this bedroom."

"You're right." My voice sounds breathless. "And we have a marriage license to get."

"Indeed, we do." Jack grins. "I should text my mom and tell her we're going to be a little later than we planned."

"Oh, it's okay. I'll do it." I reach behind me for my phone on the dresser, ignoring Jack's raised eyebrows.

My fingers fly over my screen as I type: Victoria – *Jack and I are going to be a little late. Apologies. However, I have an idea for an article for* Pink *– "Planning a Wedding in 24 Hours. Yes, It Can Be Done". Also, related, I need tomorrow off, please, and you should probably plan the same. See you soon! xo*

----

*W*ho wants to know what happens at the wedding? Or maybe the question should be, who *doesn't* want to know?

I've written a bonus chapter from Jack's point-of-view and you can get it by signing up for my email newsletter. If you're already signed up, there's no need to sign up again. You'll get the link in an upcoming newsletter.

Thank you so much for reading Jack and Angeline's story. I hope you enjoyed reading it as much as I enjoyed writing it. See you in your inbox! - Brenda xo

WHO LOVES A SECOND-CHANCE ROMANCE?

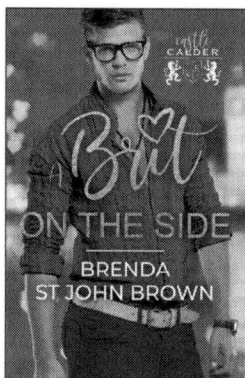

Meet Be a and Jasper

A swoony romantic comedy about getting a second chance with your best shag.

I probably should have declined my bestie's invitation to spend the summer in England working at her family's castle-turned-hotel. But, dammit, it was either that or teach summer school math. Two doors down from my ex.

Obvious choice, right?

Except now I'm living within kissing distance of Jasper for the entire summer, and he's just as sweet and sexy as I remember. Unfortunately, I also remember he gave me the best orgasm of my life in short-term parking. And on the desk chair. Then the kitchen counter. Judging by the way he kisses me, he remembers too.

Clearly, the best solution is:

a) Avoid him at all costs.

b) Sneak into Jasper's room and bring a little Atlanta heat to the UK.

c) Fall for him. Hard.

I'm not going to choose C. Almost definitely.

__Read on for chapter 1...__

A BRIT ON THE SIDE - CHAPTER 1

THERE ARE WORSE PLACES TO ESCAPE A BROKEN ENGAGEMENT than Castle Calder. I haven't even been inside yet, but when my bestie, Scarlett St Julien, pulls into the driveway of her family's castle-turned-hotel, I decide immediately. Castle Calder: one. Ex-fiancé: zero. My mother and her *Oh, but Bea, he's such a* nice *young man*: negative five hundred and eighty.

"Wow. I know you said castle, but I didn't expect, like, turrets and everything." I gape at the building in front of me. It's an honest-to-God fairy-tale castle. Big. Imposing. Regal.

Scarlett laughs, maneuvering the Ford Focus we picked up at Manchester Airport between a shiny black Range Rover and a sleek silver Audi TT. "Trust me, you'll be cursing those turrets by the time you haul a few loads of bedding down the stairs. The people who rent the turret rooms are always the ones who leave their rooms in the worst state. You don't even want to know the places I've found knickers up there."

I kind of do want to know, but Scarlett eases the car into park and opens the door in one smooth motion, hopping from her seat onto the gravel drive. I follow, leaving my door ajar as I continue to gawk at the red brick building in front of me. It looks bigger when I'm standing up. The front door alone must be eight feet tall and the windows, with their stained glass panes in the middle, are wide and sparkling in the sun.

"This is amazing." Understatement of the year. Even the cool breeze smells sweet. Judging by the thin sheen of yellow on the hood of the Audi, it's only pollen, but I have to resist calling it the perfumed air like someone out of a Regency romance. Seriously, if I could bottle this scent, I would.

"It is pretty ace, isn't it?" Scarlett grins. "Good plan?"

"Oh my God, the best." I put one hand over my heart and gesture towards the castle with the other. "And then the fair lady rescued the maiden from an awkward summer of working with her ex, whisking her across an ocean and welcoming her into her kingdom."

Scarlett giggles. "And the maiden was so beholden to the lady she wrote her thesis outline for her over the summer holiday."

I laugh. "How about, 'The maiden was so beholden to the lady, she did her laundry,' or something? It reeks more of servitude."

"I can do my own laundry. It's the outline I'm worried about. *The Impact of Color and Art in the Workplace on Employee Satisfaction* is titillating, but I need your research skills and flawless grammar."

"I'm a math teacher, not an English teacher. Remember?"

Scarlett waves her hand like she's brushing off a gnat. "Details, details. Surely a summer abroad is worth a little help with the proper use of the Oxford comma?"

"You convince my mom I'm not getting back together with Theo, let alone marrying him, and I'll Oxford comma the hell out of your outline. Swear."

"You forget I know your mother. I'll be convinced I should marry Theo by the time she's done with me." Scarlett makes a face. "Speaking of, are you ready to say hello to the motley crew we've got on here?"

"Yep." I smile, but my pulse dances a samba in my chest. I've met Scarlett's parents before, but spending Parents' Weekend with them four years ago is very different from spending the summer – especially since Scarlett convinced them to take me on as occasional help, which keeps me off the books. Truly, if I'm beholden to anyone, it's them.

Scarlett starts towards the huge front door. "We'll get our cases when we find out where you're going to be staying. Come on."

Where I'm going to be staying? Even though Scarlett said the family apartment is small and I'd be bunking elsewhere, I still half-thought I'd be in the room next to Scarlett's, connected by a too-small bathroom with a super messy counter. Just like our Atlanta apartment. Now, looking at the castle, I realize how dumb that is. This is going to be nothing like Atlanta. At all.

Scarlett pushes the front door and I follow her through, stopping immediately inside. The walls are a deep dark wood, polished and gleaming. A huge fireplace takes up most of one wall with couches placed in a semi-circle in front of it. To my right is a large antique desk with a bell sitting next to a huge vase of fresh flowers. A tapestry of a guy on a horse covers most of the wall behind the desk. He's holding a sword, a cape flying out behind him as he races towards a mountain.

"That's William," Scarlett says.

"William?"

"William the Brave."

I nod, then shrug. "I've never heard of him."

Scarlett lets out a belly laugh. "Well, technically he might be William the Wannabe. My parents got that rug at an estate auction a few years ago. I'm not sure who he is."

"Jerk." I laugh and reach out to hit her on the arm.

"Hey, I'm trying to give you the full British experience. Plus, you're the only person I know who calls me a jerk instead of a bitch and I think it's sweet." Scarlett rings the bell on the desk before continuing. "Wait until everyone starts asking you to say things. We don't get many Americans up here."

I follow as she walks through the foyer. "I've noticed."

When we stopped for gas – petrol – I ended up having a five-minute conversation with a woman in the Starbucks line after picking up the piece of paper she dropped from her bag. Once she heard my accent, we went through the gamut of questions I've heard Scarlett answer more times than I can count. Where're you from? How long are you staying? What brought you here? I've always wanted to go to New York, have you been there?

Atlanta. The summer. Vacation. And yes, but when I was five, so I don't remember much.

I haven't watched Scarlett navigate that minefield for years without learning a few things in the process. It's good to know her tactic works on both sides of the Atlantic – be slightly aloof and engage as little as possible.

Scarlett turns and grins. "I wondered if I was going to have to run interference with that woman."

"Nope, but you owe me for the 7,012 times I've done it for you, and I'm sure I'll be needing it at some point."

Starting now. A blonde girl dressed in shorts and a hoodie comes around the corner, followed closely by Mrs. Call-Me-Hannah St Julien. Both stop short before the girl throws her arms around Scarlett's neck.

"I didn't know you were already here, you numpty. Why didn't you text?"

"I emailed you our flight info. Besides, I packed my UK SIM and I have no idea where it is." Scarlett flashes a Julia Roberts smile. "And it's nice to see you, too."

The girl laughs and passes Scarlett off to her mom, who

hugs Scarlett while saying, "I was just thinking about calling to see where you were, although I guess that wouldn't have helped. I'm so glad you're here. How was your journey?"

"Good," Scarlett says into her mom's shoulder. "Tiring. You know I can never sleep on planes."

Mrs. St Julien turns to me. "And Bea, it's so lovely to see you again. Did you manage to sleep at all?"

"No. Scarlett wouldn't let me." I smile and Mrs. St Julien laughs. She gives me a quick hug, too, her arms barely circling my shoulders before she lets go. Scarlett warned me I'm going to have to get used to St Julien family hugs and calling her parents by their first names. I assured her I'm up for the challenge, but I'm glad Mrs. St Julien isn't pushing it.

"That sounds like my girl," Mrs. St Julien says. She turns to the girl in the hoodie, who's been watching our exchange. "Claire, this is Bea, Scarlett's roommate from Atlanta. They were college roommates and now Bea is a math teacher. I thought I'd put you two together out in the cabin, since Bea's going to be working in the house this summer, too."

I almost ask, "What house?" before realizing Mrs. St Julien is talking about the castle. Claire smiles at me. "I've heard a lot about you."

"Me too," I say. Instead of letting me sleep, Scarlett gave me the rundown of the summer staff at Castle Calder. Claire studies marketing at the University of Bath – pronounced Baaath – and has a crush on Will, a barman at the local pub, which, according to Scarlett, is sad and one sided. But Claire is also funny and handy with a wrench, so Will might come to his senses one of these days.

"Are you girls shattered?" Mrs. St Julien asks. "I made a lemon cake if you think you're up for it?"

Scarlett claps her hands. "My mum's lemon cake is to die for. You have to at least have a bite. Come on. I'll give you a tour on the way to the kitchen."

She walks and I follow, with Mrs. St Julien and Claire behind. We wind through hallways covered with more tapestries on the walls — but none of them are as impressive as William the Wannabe. Scarlett points out the library — full of books and a dark brown leather sofa -- and a game room — another dark brown leather sofa and a few wingback chairs -- in addition to a hallway she says I'll need to remember to access the guest rooms. I'm sincerely hoping I won't need to remember today, because wow, am I tired. Now that we're here and the excitement of the flight and being in England has abated a little, I feel every one of the thirty-six hours since I last slept.

Of course, if I hadn't left packing until the night before, I might not feel like death warmed over. *The best way to finish an unpleasant task is to get started, you know.* Ugh. Four thousand miles away and my mother's pithy sayings still follow me, if only in my head.

Scarlett pushes a door open to her left and my thoughts of home, Mom, and Atlanta stop as I follow her into the biggest kitchen I've ever seen. It's at least five times the size of mine and Scarlett's entire apartment. A silver countertop gleams along one side, but it's the wall of stoves that's most impressive. There are three huge ovens side by side and fifteen burners. Maybe more. A couple of them have pots simmering on top and there are more copper-bottomed pots stacked on the shelves than the whole kitchen department at Target.

Scarlett opens a cabinet and pulls out a stack of tea cups while Claire fills a kettle and places it on one of the stoves. It's so seamless — the way they do it without even speaking — it's clear they've done it a thousand times before.

"So, this is the kitchen," Scarlett says, grinning. To Claire and her mom, she says, "Bea's idea of cooking is chopping up tomatoes for her salad, so you may not want to let her in here unsupervised."

Claire laughs, but Mrs. St Julien shakes her head. "We're short in the kitchen this week because Emma's daughter is poorly, so, Scarlett, you'll have to fill in."

Scarlett rolls her eyes. Unlike me, she's a whiz in the kitchen, but that doesn't stop her from hating it. She survives mostly on Cup Noodle and take-out from the cheap Mexican place down the street from our apartment, but on the days she does cook, I've learned to stay out of her way. Before she can speak, I hear myself say, "I can help. I'm not as hopeless as Scarlett would have you think."

"You are, too! Remember the first time you thought you were going to make spaghetti sauce from scratch?" Scarlett says.

Mrs. St Julien holds up her hand. "Thank you, Bea. Emma helps with the prep, mostly, so if you can chop, that would be a big help."

"Plus, it beats changing the bedding," Claire says. "We have a big party coming on Friday night. Mr. Fisher's ninetieth birthday."

Between the way she says it and the way Scarlett and Mrs. St Julien's mouths purse, I'm guessing Mr. Fisher is a return guest, and not a welcome one. I'm about to ask what he's done when a deep male voice rings out behind me. "There you are. I thought I heard your voice."

Scarlett squeals and runs across the floor. My gaze follows her and lands on her target, and every thought of Mr. Fisher leaves my head as Scarlett throws her arms around the young, tall, dark-haired guy in the doorway. His sweater has a hole by the neck, his glasses are a bit askew on his face, and his chinos hang a little too loosely on his waist, but there's no denying it -- Jasper St Julien still looks damn good.

His eyes find mine over Scarlett's shoulder. They're as cool, blue, and intense as I remember and even though the whole kitchen floor stands between us, my body flushes with heat like he's standing right next to me. My stomach somersaults with the same anticipation. If Theo made me feel half of what I'm feeling right here in this suddenly too small kitchen, I'd be engaged. Happily. Willingly. But he didn't and I'm not.

For the first time since the whole Theo debacle happened, I'm glad.

AVAILABLE AT AMAZON

ABOUT THE AUTHOR

Brenda is a displaced New Yorker living in the English countryside. She's lived in the UK long enough to gain dual citizenship, but still doesn't understand Celsius. However, she has learned the appropriate use of the word "pants". And how to order a proper bacon bap/barm/buttie. Because, well, bacon.

Brenda writes contemporary romance to make you giggle and swoon. When she's not writing, she enjoys hiking, running and reading. In theory, she also enjoys cooking, but it's more that she enjoys eating and, try as she might, she can't live on Doritos alone.

I'd love for you to subscribe to my newsletter. Or if you fancy, I share lots of fun stuff in my reader Facebook group, Brenda's Book Babes.

I'd love to hear from you! Find me online here:
brendastjohnbrown.com

f 🐦 📷

ACKNOWLEDGMENTS

This book nearly didn't see the light of day. But then one day I found the old version on my laptop, along with Bev Katz Rosenblum's awesome editorial notes and thought to myself, "Hey. I can turn this into something." And here we are.

I have so many people to thank, starting with Stina Lindenblatt who always reads my words and provides invaluable insight. Thank you, too, to Marie Landry, who started off as a reviewer/blogger and has turned into one of my most trusted writer friends. Thank you both for being such amazing support!

I have to give a shout-out to my fellow RomCom Junkies. Our group chats give me life and always provide a bright spot in my day.

I'm forever in awe of how Bev Katz Rosenblum helps improve my stories by leaps and bounds. Especially this one.

Brianna Lebrecht, thank you, as always, for helping to make my book readable.

Lana Pecherczyk at Bookcoverology, my cover illustration and design is perfect!

Thank you to all of the bloggers and reviewers for all of your support. I so appreciate all that you do!

Thank you to my husband and my son for your support. I write love stories because of you. (Also, the dishwasher is RIGHT THERE.)

And thank you to all of my readers. Whether you've read all of my books or this is your first, I appreciate you taking a chance on me and my words. I hope you've enjoyed Jack and Angeline's story, and I'd love it if you would consider leaving an honest review on Amazon and/or Goodreads. Thank you in advance!

The Blind Date Diaries/ by Brenda St John Brown

1. Fiction 2. Romance 3. Contemporary

Summary: A woman writes a blind dating feature in an attempt to save her job and finds love in the process.

Cover design and illustration by Lana Pecherczyk at Bookcoverology

Editing by Bev Katz Rosenblum

Copyediting by Brianna Lebrecht

❀ Created with Vellum

Manufactured by Amazon.ca
Bolton, ON

11139715R00146